TRAVELLING MAGIC

TRAVELLING MAGIC

ELISABETH BERESFORD

Illustrated by Judith Valpy

A TARGET BOOK

published by

the Paperback Division of
W. H. ALLEN & Co. Ltd

A Target Book
Reprinted in 1977
by the Paperback Division of W. H. Allen & Co. Ltd
A Howard & Wyndham Company
123 King Street, London W6 9JG

First published in Great Britain by
Rupert-Hart Davis, Ltd, 1965,
and in this edition by
Universal-Tandem Publishing Co., Ltd, 1973

Made and printed in Great Britain
by The Anchor Press Ltd
Tiptree, Essex

ISBN 0 426 10161 8

TO

Sarah and Peter Shells

Contents

1. The House on Wandle Heights

KATE and Marcus Dawson stood huddled together at the barrier of Platform Number Two on Victoria Station and looked anxiously about them.

"Supposing she never comes?" said Kate, who had a

lively imagination and who was already starting to picture herself and her brother stranded in the middle of London.

"She will," said Marcus, who liked trains and was quite enjoying himself. "That must be the Istanbul Express over there. I wish we were on it."

"So do I," said Kate sighing heavily, "and then we could go and stay with Daddy for the holidays instead of with Miss Button."

They watched the train slowly snake its way out of the station and Kate's anxiety grew steadily as more and more people began to pour on to the platforms. They all seemed to have pale faces and worried expressions, but that could have been because it was a very dull wet day and already starting to get dark.

"Mind your backs please," a voice shouted and they had to move quickly to one side as a long luggage truck bumped past them looking rather like a great caterpillar.

"Kate? Marcus?" said a chirpy little voice. "I am Miss Button. Dear me how you've grown. Is this your luggage? Porter! Your train must have been early. Come along then, come along."

Miss Button was very small. She had neat dark hair done up in tight little curls and she was wearing a green hat and coat and carrying a rolled umbrella tucked under her arm.

"I don't think we *were* early," said Marcus, who liked to be exact about things, but Miss Button was already hurrying across the station dragging Kate with her. The porter piled their luggage into a taxi and Miss Button climbed in and leant forward, prodding the driver with the tip of her umbrella.

"Number Four, Wandle Heights," she said, "and I know the way if you're not sure of it."

"Yes, miss," the driver said and shut the little glass partition with a thud.

"I always believe in telling them that," Miss Button said nodding her head up and down energetically. "Then they know better than to try and cheat you."

"Yes," said Kate in a small voice.

It was nice to know that she and Marcus were not going to be stranded on Victoria Station after all, but Miss Button was too like some of the mistresses at school for Kate's taste and so her mouth turned even further down at the corners. Marcus didn't say anything, but he thought it would be a very brave person who would even *try* to cheat Miss Button. However, being a kind brother he understood how Kate was feeling so he gave her hand a quick squeeze for comfort.

"It's most unfortunate that your father should have been sent to Istanbul before your holidays," said Miss Button, "but you'll be very comfortable staying with my mother and myself. We take in lodgers, you know, and Mother is an excellent cook."

There didn't seem to be anything to be said in reply to that, so the two children sat in glum silence and watched the London streets bump past the windows. It had begun to rain again and the roads looked like wet liquorice while the lights were all blurred and misty. After what seemed a very long time they noticed that the taxi was

3

climbing a hill and that there seemed to be fewer houses and shops and more open space. A train roared through a cutting and they could see the engine driver's cab glowing a rosy red from the fire.

"This is the Common," said Miss Button and she leant forward and opened the glass panel and added loudly, "Right here, Cabby. Second gateway on the left."

The taxi drew up and everyone got out rather stiffly. By the orange glow of the street lamp the children could see before them the dark bulk of a large house surrounded by glinting laurel bushes all shiny from the rain. Miss Button paid the driver very slowly and carefully and he said something the children couldn't quite hear and then drove away very fast, his tyres squealing on the damp road.

"Tut!" said Miss Button. "Well, in we go. Marcus you take the large case and Kate and I will carry the others between us."

She led the way up the garden path to the front door and opened it, calling out as she did so, "Yoo-hoo. Mother, we're home."

It seemed very odd that somebody as old as Miss Button should have a mother, but the children felt too melancholy to smile. The hall in which they found themselves was large and rather chilly. There was a great deal of dark brown paint everywhere and as the wall-paper was a deep blue it was a little like being in an enormous fish tank. The feet of Marcus seemed to make an awful clatter across the stone floor and immediately two doors opened and two people appeared. They were

both old and small and Kate knew instantly that the
woman was Miss Button's mother because she looked
exactly like her, except that in Mrs Button's case all the
tight little curls were white. The man had white hair too
and a bristly moustache and a cross expression.

"How do you do?" said Mrs Button. "Dear me, *how*
you've grown. The last time I saw you, you were so
high." And she showed them exactly how high, which as
Marcus later pointed out to Kate must have made them
dwarfs.

"And what's more," added Kate, "I wish grown-up
people wouldn't always say 'How You've Grown'. They
wouldn't like it if we said 'How you've shrunk'."

"And this," said Mrs Button bustling forward, "Is
Mr Snip, who also lives here."

"How-de-do, how-de-do," said Mr Snip. "I trust
you're not always going to make such a din, heh? Heh?"

"No, sir," said Marcus.

"Well, supper in a few minutes," said Mrs Button.
"Take them up to their rooms, Doris."

"Yes, Mother," said Miss Button, "This way."

She ran lightly up the stairs, pausing on the half landing
to say over the banisters in a low voice:

"Has Mr Trevellick arrived yet?"

"He has indeed," said Mr Snip suddenly reappearing
in the hall, "And a very odd sort of man he is too."

"Odd in what way?" Miss Button asked in alarm.

"Peculiar," Mr Snip replied unhelpfully and stumped
back into the sitting room again and shut the door.

"Oh dear," said Miss Button, resuming her journey.

"Mr Trevellick is another new lodger who's come to stay with us. He was due to arrive today. I wonder what Mr Snip can have meant?"

"It's going to be a horrible holiday and I wish we weren't here," said Kate ten minutes later. "There's cross old Mr Snip and peculiar Mr Trevellick and everybody's old and I hate it." Her voice rose to a wobbly note and Marcus said hastily:

"Don't cry."

"Who's crying?" said Kate, who was doing exactly that. "What are you looking at?"

"The garden."

Marcus moved aside the curtain and Kate, still sniffing went to join him. By the light from the window they could see little silver arrows of rain darting through the blackness and beyond them some bare trees which were miserably rubbing their branches together as though they didn't like being wet.

"It's not much of a garden," said Kate, who was now determined to look on the black side of everything at Wandle Heights.

"There's another garden on the other side of the wall," said Marcus, peering out into the night. "And at least it'll be something to explore."

"Supper," said Miss Button, putting her head round the door. "I'm afraid you won't be able to see much at this time of night, but tomorrow you can go out and have a look round the Common."

"What about the garden down there?" Marcus asked pointing.

"That's called the Triangle, because it's three-sided," Miss Button explained. "It's surrounded by the other houses on Wandle Heights and you can only get to it through the back gardens. It was very nicely kept at one time I believe, but now people just use it to dump their rubbish. It's not at all the place for you to go and play in. Have you washed your hands?"

"Just as though we were babies," Marcus grumbled under his breath. But as they were both very hungry their spirits rose a little as they went down the stairs and a delicious smell of stew reached their noses. Miss Button showed them into the dining room where Mr Snip was already sitting at the table with his white hair carefully brushed and a hopeful expression on his face.

"It's one minute past seven," he said, looking at a large silver watch.

"Dear me, so it is," said Miss Button. "I won't be a moment." She left the room and they heard her speak to somebody in the hall and then the door opened again and Miss Button, looking rather flustered, reappeared with a tall thin young man who had a very sunburnt face and bright blue eyes. Afterwards both Marcus and Kate were quite sure that they had both noticed something strangely different about him right from that very first minute. It wasn't only his rather unusual suit of thick nobbly cloth or his haircut which looked as if he had had a pudding basin put over his head and then somebody had chopped away round the rim with a pair of blunt shears. It was just something about him personally.

"This is Mr Trevellick," said Miss Button, "——Kate

Dawson, Mr Snip, Marcus Dawson. I'll get the supper."

"How-de-do, how de-do?" said Mr Snip.

Mr Trevellick half raised his arm as though he was about to make a salute and then changed his mind and bobbed his head instead. He seemed to be extremely nervous and Kate wondered if he was very shy.

"Well sit down, sit down," said Mr Snip as Mr Trevellick moved uneasily from foot to foot in the doorway.

"Thank you," said Mr Trevellick hastily and then cleared his throat. He spoke very slowly and with a pleasant west-country drawl in his voice.

"Staying here long?" asked Mr Snip who was obviously curious about this new guest.

"I am not certain," said Mr Trevellick. "I have work to do and do not know how long it will take."

"What sort of work?" said Mr Snip.

Mr Trevellick laced his fingers together and cracked his knuckles in a way that instantly won Marcus' admiration. He had always wanted to learn to do that trick himself.

"I am studying for a degree," said Mr Trevellick more huskily than ever. He looked up with relief as Miss Button came in with a tray which she put down in front of Mr Snip.

"Lamb cutlet stew," she said. "Perhaps you'd be kind enough to serve, Mr Snip?"

She left the room quickly and Mr Snip began to ladle out the food. As Marcus and Kate both felt very shy and Mr Trevellick apparently didn't like talking, Mr Snip was the only one to speak. He rambled on from subject to subject, always coming back to the same topic which was that nothing these days was as good as it used to be.

"Why in my young days," said Mr Snip as everybody else ate steadily in silence, "even the weather was better. The sun used to shine then and it was warm in the summer. Not like it is now. Heh?"

"No sir," said Marcus as this last 'heh' was directed at him.

"*You* don't know anything about it," Mr Snip said ufnairly. "*You* weren't born."

Kate was only half listening to all this for she was watching Mr Trevellick with growing interest. She had never before seen anybody hold a knife and fork so awkwardly and then to her utter astonishment Mr Trevellick picked up a lamb bone in his fingers and began to chew it.

"When I was young," began Mr Snip and then he became aware of Kate's amazed stare and turned to have a look at Mr Trevellick himself.

"Good gracious!" said Mr Snip.

Mr Trevellick finished the bone, which was now quite clean and with a satisfied sigh threw it neatly over his shoulder. Kate gave a hastily muffled gurgle of laughter, Marcus choked and Mr Snip went quite purple in the face. Miss Button chose this unlucky moment to come into the room and her eyebrows rose right up into her curls as she looked from the bone to the amazed faces of the others. There was a moment's quite awful silence and then Mr Trevellick pushed back his chair, muttered

9

something and dashed out of the room. They listened to his footsteps thudding up the stairs and then a door at the top of the house was shut.

"Dear me," Miss Button said faintly, "Dear, *dear* me. A dustpan and brush. It's orange jellies for pudding made from real fruit juice," and she hurried out again.

"Nothing is the same any more," said Mr Snip frowning terribly at poor Kate who was now unable to control her laughter. "Not even good manners it seems."

"I couldn't help it, I just couldn't," said Kate shakily when fifteen minutes later she and Marcus escaped to her bedroom. "When we first got here I thought I was never going to smile again——just like the king in history, you know the one I mean——and then I was frightened I was never going to stop. I've got the most awful stitch."

"I think it was Henry the First," said Marcus, who liked to take things step by step. "And come to that, I believe it was Henry the Eighth who always threw chicken bones over his shoulder. I saw him do it in a film once. He is odd isn't he?"

"Who, Henry the . . ."

"No, Mr Trevellick, stupid."

"Yes, odd but nice. Perhaps he's been living on some long lost island as a hermit and he's forgotten how to behave."

"I don't think there are any hermits now," Marcus said cautiously. "I hope he stays though. He's better than cross old Mr Snip."

"I don't suppose Miss Button'll *let* him stay," Kate said sighing. "She's one of those very tidy people and I'm sure she doesn't like guests who throw their bones on the carpet."

Kate was still smiling about the scene in the dining-room when she went to sleep and Marcus too was feeling quite cheerful as he drifted off in the bedroom next door. He was in the middle of a very interesting dream about playing football at school when there was a thudding noise on his window.

"S' a goal," Marcus said sleepily turning over and snuggling further down into his nice warm bed. The window-pane rattled again and there was an angry squawking followed by a slithering sound.

"Who is it? Kate?" said Marcus sitting up and reaching for the switch of his bedside light. But the room was quite empty and after a moment he was just deciding that he had woken up for nothing when the slithering began again. Marcus' heart banged in his chest, for noises in the middle of the night in a strange house can be very un-settling. He took a deep breath and got out of bed and crept across to the window and twitched back the curtain. At first he couldn't see anything and then as his eyes got used to the darkness he was able to make out a small hunched shape perched miserably on the sill. Two angry yellow eyes slowly opened and stared up into his own.

"Why——it's an owl," Marcus said to the empty bed-room.

2. *Horace*

"Who? Why? What?" said Kate.

"Shh," Marcus said and put his hand over her mouth.

"MMph," Kate said wetly into his palm.

"If you promise not to make a row I'll explain," Marcus said in a whisper. Kate nodded so he took his hand away and sat down on the edge of her bed.

"There's an owl in my room," Marcus said.

"You didn't wake me up just to tell me that did you?" Kate said crossly, for like most people she was never in a good temper if she was woken suddenly.

"Oh well, of course, if you're not interested go back to sleep," Marcus said. "Only I thought you might like to see it."

He crept out of her bedroom and went softly back to his own room where the owl was still miserably crouched on the window-sill. It's feathers were all ruffled and the yellow eyes had a dull expression about them. However, its small, curving beak looked as if it could peck quite painfully so Marcus didn't get too close.

"Poor little bird," said Kate, tiptoeing into the room, "What's the matter then?"

The owl slowly shut its eyes and ruffled its feathers still further. Kate put out a gentle hand and carefully stroked it and the bird didn't seem to object although it edged a little further up the sill.

"I think it's ill," Kate said. She was very fond of animals and would have liked to have had a pet of her own. On one occasion she had smuggled a mouse back to school, but unfortunately it had escaped from its snug little house in her locker in the middle of a dull French lesson. The French mistress had not been at all fond of mice, it soon transpired, and after ten extremely noisy minutes the mouse had escaped, the Mademoiselle had been escorted back to the staff room by the Matron for a soothing cup of tea and Kate had been sent to the Headmistress. All this flashed through her mind now and she said, "Couldn't we keep it, secretly?"

"We could try I suppose," Marcus said doubtfully.

"Hoooo," the owl said. It was not a very loud noise, but in the middle of the silent house it sounded like a small factory hooter.

"Shh," Marcus and Kate said together.

The owl gave them another baleful glare from its yellow eyes and launched itself off the window-sill and into the night. Kate gave a cry of disappointment and ran to watch it as it swooped across the sky which was a strange orange colour because of the street lamps.

"What a shame," Kate said, sighing deeply.

"Yes," agreed Marcus not quite truthfully as he had thought that the owl might have made a difficult and perhaps even a dangerous pet. He was about to move away from the window when Kate said in a strange, breathless voice, "Look——look at the Triangle."

Marcus screwed up his eyes and peered through the orange mist. Beyond it he could see dimly some tall trees and a little stream which shimmered in the moonlight before it vanished under a small stone bridge. On either side of the water there were still white figures which glimmered, and beyond them was a fountain and a weeping willow whose branches swayed between the fat green leaves of water lilies.

"It's beautiful," whispered Kate, clasping her hands together. "It's the most beautiful garden I've ever seen.

It's even better than Hampton Court. But what are those people doing? Why don't they move?"

"They're statues," Marcus said slowly. "But Kate, the garden didn't look like this when we saw it this afternoon."

"Perhaps we didn't see it properly," said Kate who was now nearly half-way out of the window in her excitement. Marcus took a careful grip on the back of her dressing-gown and shook his head.

"It just wasn't there," he said firmly.

"Well it is now," Kate replied. "We must go and explore it tomorrow. Oh I wish it was morning now."

"And what," said a stern voice from the doorway, "is the meaning of this, may I ask?"

Both children turned round with a guilty jump and saw Miss Button watching them. She was wearing a pink quilted dressing-gown, fluffy pink slippers and a large number of uncomfortable looking curlers in her hair. Her face was pale and her expression cross.

Kate slipped behind Marcus for comfort and he said quickly:

"It was my fault. The owl woke me up and I went in to tell Kate about it."

"Owl?" said Miss Button, her eyebrows rising up as high as the curlers. "There are no owls here."

"It's gone now, but it was here, honestly," Kate said over her brother's shoulder. "I think it was ill."

"I see," said Miss Button in the kind of voice which made it quite plain that she saw nothing of the sort. Kate, who didn't like having her word doubted, became a little braver and she went on quickly, "And then when it flew away we saw the Triangle."

"Well naturally," said Miss Button in faint astonishment, "If you looked out of the window that's exactly what you would see."

"We think it's beautiful," Kate said. "Can't we go and play in it please?"

"Certainly not," Miss Button replied, "I've already told you it's quite unsuitable. Now off to bed with you, Kate, and let's have no more wandering about in the middle of the night. You'll catch cold."

"Please, Miss Button," said Kate. "It is a lovely garden ——the Triangle, I mean. Why can't we play there?"

"What is the matter with the child?" Miss Button said, as though she was talking to herself. "Here it is one o'clock in the morning and a very busy day ahead. As though I hadn't enough . . ."

"Just look at it," Kate pleaded. Miss Button hesitated and then crossed over to the window and jerked aside the curtain.

"And what," she said crossly, "is so pretty about that, may I ask?"

Kate and Marcus stared out into the misty orange gloom. Little silver arrows of rain were still darting towards the ground and beyond them were the quiet bare trees and the crumbling brick wall, and on the other side of that were more trees and some dark tangled grass and a few stunted bushes. It was a sad damp scene and there was no sign at all of the marble statues and the tinkling little stream with its bridge and willow tree. All that had vanished as if it had never existed and both Marcus and Kate felt a cold shiver run up the entire length of their respective backs.

"You see," said Miss Button.

"But we did——there was——" said Kate.

"You've been dreaming," Miss Button said more kindly. "Oddly enough, when I was about your age I used to have dreams about the Triangle sometimes. I was very fanciful as a child." She sighed and her face stopped being cross and anxious for a moment and then she straightened her shoulders and said, "Now off to bed, both of you. And I don't want to hear another word about owls or gardens or anything else for that matter. Come along, Kate."

She took Kate by the arm and marched her to the door. Kate looked over her shoulder at Marcus who was still standing by the window with a surprised expression on his face. He caught Kate's eye and gave her a small wink so she didn't say anything, but obediently followed Miss Button out of the room. Marcus slowly lifted the curtain and looked down at the sooty window-sill and there, on the very edge, were some small smudged claw marks.

"Well, the owl was real anyway," said Marcus to the wet dark night.

All the same when the morning arrived, and he and Kate had got dressed and washed, the happenings of the night before did seem very like a dream. They discussed it in low voices until the sound of the gong booming in the hall reminded them that it was breakfast time. Mr Snip was hidden behind a large newspaper and he just looked over the top of it for a moment and growled "Good morning" and then disappeared again. Mr Trevellick was late and he too looked as if he had had a disturbed night for there were shadows under his bright blue eyes. He smiled shyly at the children and slipped into his chair.

"Ha, Ha!" said Mr Snip suddenly reappearing round the side of his newspaper, "Sleep well?"

"Yes, thank you," said Mr Trevellick. He didn't begin eating until after the others and then he chewed every mouthful very slowly and deliberately. As Miss Button seemed to be in a great hurry Kate offered to help carry out the dirty plates and cups.

"That would be kind," said Miss Button. "It's always such a rush in the mornings."

Kate followed her down the long dark passage to the kitchen where Mrs Button was having her breakfast. It was a large room with a dresser running along one wall and an old fashioned boiler standing in an alcove on the opposite side. It would have been very dark if the light hadn't been on, as the window looked directly onto the side of the next door house.

"Off you go, Doris," said Mrs Button getting stiffly to her feet. "Well Kate, I hear you were wandering about the house half the night."

"I didn't wander very far," Kate said.

"Imagining you heard an owl, indeed," said Mrs Button, "I've lived here for seventy years and I've never heard one."

Kate didn't know what to say to that, so she wisely

held her tongue and escaped back to the dining-room where Mr Snip was saying almost exactly the same thing to Marcus.

"An owl? An owl? So that's what you were all jabbering about. Never heard such nonsense. Starlings, yes; nasty noisy birds they are too, and those fat greedy pigeons, we've got plenty of *them*. I tried to grow some runner-beans one summer. They stole the lot. Stole the lot."

"An owl," said Mr Trevellick in his soft slow voice. "So that's what——" he hesitated and fiddled with his tea-cup. "So that's what the noise was about."

Marcus was quite sure that he had been going to say something else and had then changed his mind. Mr Trevellick swallowed down the rest of his tea, made a face as though he hadn't much cared for the taste and then with a nod of his head left the room.

"Strange fellow that," said Mr Snip. "Secretive. Well, what are you two going to do with yourselves, eh? Go owl-hunting?" He gave a wheezy sound which might have been a laugh and picked up his newspaper and stumped out.

"We'll explore," Marcus said to Kate, "as soon as Mrs Button leaves the kitchen. There must be a side way through to the garden and then we'll be able to have a proper look at the Triangle."

They went and sat in the back sitting-room until they heard Mrs Button go past in the passage and up the stairs. Then very quietly they made their way to the kitchen and out through the scullery door into the garden. It was decidedly cold and Kate wished that she had brought her coat with her. It was a long narrow garden with a humpy gravel path down one side, a patchy lawn and several rather tired bushes which had a discouraged air about them, as if they had long ago given up the struggle to survive in the sooty London air.

Down at the bottom there was an iron gate which was almost covered by ivy. Marcus parted the shiny wet leaves and looked through to the Triangle. It was quite large and something about it suddenly made Marcus feel very sad. It seemed as though it had been forgotten and left to wither away without anybody caring what happened to it. The long tangled grass was full of rusty tins and sodden cardboard packets, and under one of the trees was an old rolled up mattress covered in dark stains and patches. There were no birds, nor sign of life, and the whole place seemed to be holding its breath.

"Oh," said Kate, who had burrowed in beside Marcus, "oh, the poor Triangle. We must have dreamt what it used to be like. What a shame that people let it get like this."

"We didn't dream it," Marcus said. "We couldn't both dream the *same* dream."

"Then what did we do?" Kate asked reasonably.

"I don't know," Marcus said, scratching his head. "Come on, we'd better get back before someone spots us and we get into more trouble. Let's go and have a look at the suitable Common."

The Common was very large and well cared for and rather dull. It stretched like a flat damp carpet for nearly

a mile and round its edges were rows and rows of small
brick houses which all looked exactly alike. Behind them
were some enormous cranes swinging slowly backwards
and forwards as they knitted up a great towering block of
flats. The only thing that interested Marcus was the railway cutting. He would quite liked to have stayed there,
watching the short suburban trains rushing about their
business; but Kate was feeling cold, so after a while they
went back to Wandle Heights.

The immediate thing they noticed as soon as they got
up to the first floor was the faint bitter smell which
seemed to be drifting down the stairs.

"It's like fireworks that have gone wrong," said Kate.

"Let's go and find out," said Marcus who was in an
exploring mood.

They listened to see if anybody was about, but the only
sound was the muffled hum of a vacuum cleaner, so they
climbed cautiously upwards. The top landing had a great
deal of dark brown paint and the wallpaper pattern here
was of red roses which had faded and gone patchy. There
was linoleum on the floor, and although they tried not to
make any noise Marcus' shoes, as they always did, seemed
determined to clatter. They followed the smell like two
eager puppies, and it was easy to discover that it came
from the very last doorway.

"You can even see it," said Kate, which was quite true
as a thin wisp of green smoke was sliding under the door.

"Perhaps something's on fire," said Marcus and
knocked.

There was a bump inside the room and then some

muttering and finally Mr Trevellick's voice said anxiously:
"Who is it?"

"Us," said Marcus, "I mean Marcus and Kate."

A key was turned and the door was opened a few inches
and instantly the bitter smell became a great deal stronger.
Kate choked and got out her handkerchief to cover her
nose.

"Is anything wrong?" Marcus asked, his eyes watering.

Mr Trevellick didn't reply for a moment, but just stood
there cracking his knuckles, his blue eyes full of worry.
Then he appeared to make up his mind about something
for he stood back and threw the door wide open. Marcus
and Kate walked in slowly, not quite knowing what to
expect, but it was only a very ordinary bedroom if rather
shabbily furnished. In front of the fire was a small gas
ring and on this was a cheap saucepan full of a dark green
liquid which bubbled and steamed. It was quite obvious
now where the unpleasant smell was coming from.

"Are you trying to cook something?" Kate asked
through her handkerchief.

"Well not exactly," said Mr Trevellick cracking his
knuckles one after the other. "I was hoping to make a
potion. I managed to collect all the right ingredients,
though I must say it wasn't easy, but something must
have got mixed in with them. It's not at all as it should
be."

"Are you ill?" asked Kate, adding, "If I were you I
should open the window. If Mrs Button smells your
medicine she'll come up to find out what's happened."

"Is it as bad as that?" exclaimed Mr Trevellick, "Dear

me!" He did as Kate suggested and the green smoke began to trail out into the cold grey morning sky. "No I'm not ill," he went on, "but Horace is far from well. I daresay it was the journey. Between ourselves," he lowered his voice, "I think he's getting too old to travel great distances."

"Who's Horace?" asked Marcus, wondering if there was yet another lodger at Wandle Heights whom they hadn't met.

To his surprise Mr Trevellick, instead of replying, got down on his hands and knees and looked under the bed.

"You'd better come out," Mr Trevellick said. "I'm sure they'll not betray us, will you?" he asked.

"No," said Kate and Marcus together, and Marcus added, "Rather not. But isn't it rather a tight squeeze getting somebody under there? Oh!"

For it was not a person who emerged from under the bed, but a small bedraggled figure whom he instantly recognised.

"It's my owl," Marcus said.

"Not yours," Mr Trevellick contradicted. "Mine. Only on loan of course."

"And you call him Horace?" Marcus said.

"Oh no, no indeed," replied Mr. Trevellick sitting down on the bed and picking up the owl and stroking its ragged feathers. "I didn't call him that. He chose the name himself."

"But owls can't talk," Kate said. "Parrots can, and some budgerigars, but not owls. Honestly, Mr Trevellick."

The bird slowly blinked its weary yellow eyes and then opening its sharp little beak, made a gulping noise, rather as if it had whooping cough.

"There, there," said Mr Trevellick, gently patting its heaving back with two fingers. "Never mind. If the potion is no use I shall have to try a spell instead. The only trouble is that I'm not really very good at that kind of thing yet. We shall just have to hope that I get the words right, that's all. Are you ready, Horace?"

The owl bowed its head and Mr Trevellick, frowning fiercely, began to mutter in Latin.

3. Mr Trevellick Talks

"It's no good," Mr Trevellick said wretchedly. "I
haven't got as far as Advanced Spells yet and I don't
suppose I ever *will* with the mess I've made of
things already. But crying over spilt mead won't help

25

Horace. He really can talk you know, when he's well."

"Yes, of course," said Marcus politely.

For the last ten minutes Mr Trevellick had been muttering to himself and waving his hands over the owl, but Horace had remained obstinately silent apart from an occasional cough. Kate was very disappointed, but Marcus who didn't believe in spells, had never imagined that anything *would* happen.

"You don't believe me, I can see," Mr Trevellick said sadly. "Couldn't you make a great effort, Horace, just for me?" The owl shook out its feathers, coughed deeply and then, fixing its eyes firmly on Marcus it said huskily:

"*Credite!*"

"There," Mr Trevellick said, cracking his knuckles as the children stared round-eyed. "I'm afraid when he's upset he'll only speak in Latin and as he's not overfond of—— er —— young people that's probably made him cross too. I'm deeply ashamed of not admitting that Horace is staying here with me. But I was afraid that if Miss Button discovered I had brought him into her house, she might not let him stay."

"It doesn't matter," Marcus said. "And *I'm* sorry I didn't believe you. I'm awfully glad we didn't dream him too, like the garden."

"The garden?" said Mr Trevellick sharply.

"Well, it's like this: last night . . ." said Marcus and poured out the whole story ending with, "I suppose you'll think that we've made it all up, but it really is true and it was the most super garden we've ever seen. But today it's vanished. It just isn't *there* any more."

"Oh no, it's still there," Mr Trevellick said. "For those who have eyes to see it."

"You mean you've seen it too?" Marcus asked in astonishment.

"In a way. I travelled through the garden to get to Wandle Heights. That's why I came here in the first place, because of the garden. I had a very difficult time getting past the kitchen. Mrs Button was washing dishes in the sink," said Mr Trevellick.

"It's no good, I don't understand what you're talking about," Marcus said rubbing his hot forehead.

Before Mr Trevellick could explain further Horace gave a small dry cough. It seemed to catch in his throat for he certainly made a most frightening noise as though he were being choked.

"Oh never mind the garden now," Kate said. "We must do something to help Horace. What's in the medicine you've been giving him, Mr Trevellick?"

"Leaf of the laurel, bark of the chestnut gathered at midnight——and you've no notion how difficult *that* was to do——grass and seed of the apple," said Mr Trevellick ticking the items off on his long fingers. "It's a perfectly well known and tested remedy and I have made use of it many, many times before. But the bark had a strange smell to it; perhaps that is why it's gone wrong."

"Well I've never heard of a medicine like that," said Marcus. "But then we just get ours at the chemist on a doctor's prescription. I expect it was soot or petrol fumes on the bark."

"Horace hasn't touched any of it," said Mr Trevellick. He looked helplessly at Kate who said briskly:

"We must find a pet shop and ask them what to do. You'd better keep him warm, and Marcus and I'll go straight out after lunch."

"I don't like to trouble you," said Mr Trevellick, "but I should be most grateful for your help. It is all so different from what I expected."

"I wonder what he did expect and where he's come *from?*" said Kate when an hour later she and Marcus were walking across the flat empty Common.

"I want to know what he meant about the garden," Marcus said. "And I do wish I'd learnt more Latin. I can only remember *amo, amas, amat,* and that's not much good. The master at school's always saying how useful Latin is, but I never believed him till now."

"Horace is a bit like Mr Snip in a way," Kate said, skipping to keep up with Marcus who was walking faster and faster, "because I don't think Mr Snip likes children much either. But at least he does talk English to us."

They had reached the edge of the Common by now and they paused by the zebra crossing until there was a gap in the heavy traffic which was racing along the main road as though each driver was in a desperate hurry. At last one lorry slowed down for them and waved them over the road. There was a small straggling line of shops here, and after they had passed a butcher's, a grocer's and, rather more slowly, a sweetshop, they were lucky enough to find one with *H. Green, Pets* over the door.

Marcus pushed it open and they went inside. As the door
shut behind them the noise of the traffic gave way to quite
a different sound which was made up of dogs barking,
birds singing and a Siamese cat with blue eyes which
yawned and then cried like a baby.

"Oh, aren't they sweet? Oh look! Oh!" said Kate
ecstatically, going from cage to cage. "Oh I do wish I
could have a pet. I'd love one of those dear little puppies,
or that tiny kitten, or even a bird."

"Well you can't," Marcus said hastily. A woman came
out of the back room and shuffled towards them. She
had a face a little like a parrot and she had an open book
in her hand. It was obviously a very interesting book as
she looked quite annoyed at being interrupted.

"Yes?" she said.

"We'd like an owl medicine, please," Marcus said.

The woman closed the book with a snap and peered at
him suspiciously over the top of her spectacles.

"Are you trying to be funny, young man?" she asked.

"No," said Marcus stolidly. "I know an owl and it's
not well and it needs some medicine."

"Well I dunno I'm sure," the woman said rather helplessly. She looked along the crowded shelves where
brightly coloured packets of seeds and fat little bags of
sand stood shoulder to shoulder with biscuits, rubber
bones and plastic birds.

"Budgerigar tonic be all right?" she asked.

"I should think so," Marcus said. "How——um——
much?"

"Tenpence ha'penny, and a bargain at the price," the

woman said. She took down a tiny bottle which was full of a dark brown liquid and rubbed the dust off it on the sleeve of her overall. It seemed that other customers did not think it all that much of a bargain.

Marcus paid up and dragged Kate away from a box where five puppies were sleepily tumbling all over one another. The woman watched them go, then opened her book again and shuffled into the back room.

Mr Trevellick was sitting on the bed when they returned. Horace, wrapped in something which resembled a loosely knitted sock, was on his lap and appeared to be very sorry for himself. Mr Trevellick was even more absent-minded than usual and for a moment or two he hardly seemed to recognise the children at all.

"It doesn't smell much better than your medicine," Marcus said, unscrewing the little stopper and sniffing, "but it says on the side of the bottle that it's guaranteed to 'restore Budgies' plumage'."

"Does it?" said Mr Trevellick doubtfully. "I'm so sorry, I don't quite understand. What is budgie?"

"It's short for budgerigar," Marcus explained, carefully measuring out three drops into Mr Trevellick's toothmug and adding a small amount of water. "Now come on, Horace."

Horace turned his head away, but after a minute or so while Mr Trevellick whispered to him and smoothed down the ruffled feathers the bird reluctantly opened its small beak. The moment it had finished drinking Mr Trevellick put his fingers round the beak and kept it firmly shut.

"You're not to spit it out," he ordered. The owl glared at him furiously and Mr Trevellick for the first time since the children had met him actually laughed.

"Poor Horace, he's been grumbling ever since he arrived," he said. "First the journey upset him and then when we did get here he said it was so noisy. He's not used to your traffic you know, and then the final blow was the street lighting. He says that bright orange blinds him so that he can't see where he's going. That's how he landed up on your window-sill by mistake."

"I think he's going to sleep," Kate said.

Mr Trevellick laid the little bird gently on the pillow and moved over to the shabby old armchair in front of the fire. He had taken his green medicine off the gas-ring and it had nearly stopped smelling, although it still looked extremely nasty.

"And now," said Mr Trevellick, "I think I should explain myself."

"You don't have to you know," Marcus said rather uncomfortably. He wasn't used to grown-up people explaining their actions to him.

"I would rather do so," Mr Trevellick said gently. "You have been so very kind. The truth of the matter is, I don't belong here at all."

"Well, we did rather guess that," Kate said as politely as she could.

"Oh dear, does it show that much?" said Mr Trevellick, furrowing up his forehead under the odd hair-cut. "I trained so hard for the journey. No, I belong in the Sixth Century. A.D. of course," he added as an afterthought.

Not surprisingly, this remark produced nothing but an astonished silence. He had said it so calmly, in just the kind of way that a stranger might have remarked, "I've come from Cheltenham——or Liverpool——or Broadstairs."

"That's a time, not a place," Marcus said at last.

"You can't *really* have one without the other," Mr Trevellick replied, "although my home is in this country ——but a little further to the West. You call it Cornwall now."

"Hold on a minute," said Marcus, putting his hands over his eyes in an attempt to try and think clearly. "People just don't come from times."

"You came from yesterday," Mr Trevellick said triumphantly, "otherwise you wouldn't be here today."

"That's different," was all Marcus could manage after several moments very hard and confused thinking which left him feeling as though his head was going round in circles. Kate had quite given up trying to follow the conversation and was sitting quietly on the floor, watching Mr Trevellick with interest and wondering if he could persuade Horace to speak to them again.

"Yes, you're right, it wasn't quite fair of me," Mr Trevellick agreed, his blue eyes twinkling. "I took a short cut."

"Through fourteen centuries?" Marcus asked in amazement.

"It seemed like a lot more than that," Mr Trevellick replied sighing. "It's the longest journey I've ever done and that's why they sent Horace with me. He's travelled all over the place. Egypt in the fourth century B.C.) he says he met the Phoenix there but I've never quite believed him), China two hundred years after that. He was in America before Christopher Columbus was even born *and* he was sent as an observer to the Great Fire of London."

"*Sixteen sixty-six*," Kate said suddenly. "*London burnt like dry sticks*. That's an easy one to remember."

"All right," said Marcus trying to make his imagination stretch to take in all this extraordinary information. "If you say he did . . ."

"And I forgot Rome," Mr Trevellick interrupted snapping his fingers. "That's where he picked up his present name you know. He's always had a great respect for the famous philosopher since then. I'm sorry——you were saying?"

"Why are you here?" Marcus asked, sticking doggedly to the point as usual.

"I'm on a month's course. Actually it's a sort of travelling scholarship into the future," Mr Trevellick replied. "I have to study your living and working conditions. Housing, Food, and Transport, and, I hope," here he crossed his fingers, "I shall get my degree and be admitted as a full member of my Circle."

"What's that?" asked Marcus.

"The Magicians' and Associated Trades," Mr Trevellick said proudly. "Some people call it MAT for short."

"You mean you're a magician?" Kate asked breathlessly. She had only met one once before, and he had been a tubby little man in a dark suit who had done wonderful tricks at a Christmas Party. He had been quite different from Mr Trevellick.

"Only an apprentice," Mr Trevellick said modestly. "It takes years and years of studying to get to the top of the profession. My family is a very humble one and they have made considerable sacrifices to pay for my training. That is why my getting this scholarship has been such a great help. Alas, I'm afraid they will be very disappointed in me."

"Why?" Kate and Marcus asked in the same breath.

Mr Trevellick glanced at Horace who was now snoring steadily on the pillow, his small beak lifting every so often as he snorted.

"*He* was to have acted as my advisor," Mr Trevellick whispered, "He has such great experience, you see. But I think that he's become a little old for the job, and without him to guide me I fear that I may make some terrible mistakes."

"Yes, I daresay you will," Kate said candidly, thinking of the bones in the lamb stew.

A rather gloomy silence fell over the three of them. Marcus stared at the spluttering gas fire, thinking over all the extraordinary things that Mr Trevellick had just told them. Kate absent-mindedly took the saucepan over to the wash-basin and began to clean it with a nail-brush and Mr Trevellick went to the window and gazed out at the Triangle.

"What did you mean about the garden?" Marcus asked suddenly.

"The Wandle Heights Triangle?" said Mr Trevellick,

"It is one of the few enchanted pieces of land left in this country. There used to be dozens of them, all over the place. They were started by one of the earliest——and most powerful——of our Circle, in the Fifth Century. Shortly after the Romans left you know, and the Barbarians started to arrive. This particular magician felt that they would come in very useful in times of danger or trouble. Of course there *were* earlier ones——Stone Henge for instance——but it was very crude in spite of all the hard work they put into it."

"What are they used for?" Marcus asked.

"Travelling," Mr Trevellick said simply. "We use them in much the same way as you use buses or railway trains. Most of them have been built over now though ——you have so many houses and factories and roads. This is one of the few left in the London area."

"It seems a very odd place to have it," Kate said doubtfully.

"Not at all. It's on high ground, so one can see one's enemies coming. It is only a mere two miles from the Thames, and when it was first formed there were several small villages round about which needed protection from local tribes and, of course, later on, from the Vikings who came plundering up this way."

"But why can't people see it?" Marcus asked.

"They could if they wanted to. However, in your modern world all the people appear to be either in a great hurry, or extremely anxious, or just too busy to take the trouble to look for it."

"We saw it," said Kate.

"Ah, that's a gift that quite a number of children have. Unfortunately they lose it as they grow older. I hope *you* never will," Mr Trevellick added smiling at her.

Marcus joined Mr Trevellick at the window and looked out into the dusk. The orange street lights were switched on and the air was full of damp yellow mist. An idea began to form in Marcus' mind and as it did so he saw the bare wet trees in the Triangle tremble and fade away and in their place there came into view the gleaming marble statues and the little tinkling stream. It was almost like watching a play on television, only far, far better because it was all in colour and it was real.

"Kate," said Marcus. "Come here."

They stood side by side and he knew without looking at her that she too could see the Triangle properly.

"Mr Trevellick," Marcus said huskily, "couldn't *we* help you instead of Horace doing it?"

"I really don't know," Mr Trevellick said helplessly. "It's very kind of you, but I've never come across this situation before."

"Think of your poor anxious family," Kate said.

"What about your travelling scholarship?" Marcus asked.

The gong down in the hall boomed out for the evening meal.

"Supper. Wash your hands," called Miss Button's voice.

"Please," said Kate.

Mr Trevellick cracked his fingers, ruffled his hair so

that it stood up on end and looked odder than ever and then let out a deep sigh of relief.

"Thank you," he said. "Thank you for your very generous offer which it gives me great pleasure to accept."

"Sup——per," Miss Button called on a high note. "Come along now, it's getting cold."

4. *The Enchanted Garden*

"THE thing is," said Marcus, "I really don't know much about Housing. I mean houses are just there, and people live in them."

"Or in flats," Kate said helpfully.

"How do people get into them if they're flat?" asked Mr Trevellick, looking up from a little notebook which Mrs Button had given him and in which he had been writing busily. Neither Marcus nor Kate could read his script which looked more like the footprints of small birds than real writing.

"They're not flat that way," said Kate putting her hand level with the table. "They go up like this," and she pointed her fingers to the ceiling.

"Then why are they called flat?" said Mr Trevellick in a despairing voice.

"Because they're built flat one on top of each other I suppose," Marcus replied. "But it'd be much easier if we could just show you."

He was longing to go into the Triangle, but all three of them had had to wait for Mrs Button to come out of the kitchen. For once it was quite a nice morning with a pale sun which looked like a sucked acid-drop. Horace, who still refused to speak to the children, was a little better, but was spending the day on the top shelf of the cupboard in Mr Trevellick's bedroom.

"Hah," said Mr Snip, appearing in the doorway. "Not going out? When I was young we were made to take walks every day, but things were different then."

"Different in what way, sir?" asked Mr Trevellick politely.

Mr Snip marched over to the best armchair, sat down and opened the paper with an angry rustle.

"Better," he said from behind the pages. "Much, much better. I'll trouble you not to talk when I'm reading."

There were footsteps on the stairs and Marcus beckoned to the other two and led them out into the passage.

"I wonder why he's always so cross," Kate whispered as they tiptoed through the empty kitchen.

"I believe he has a great worry," Mr Trevellick replied. "In our tribes the old people are honoured and respected for their years and their knowledge, so they are happy and contented. It seems to me that in your modern times life is difficult for those who are no longer young. Mrs Button has to work and Mr Snip . . ."

"What about him?" said Marcus opening the scullery door.

"I don't know what troubles him yet," Mr Trevellick said thoughtfully.

They walked quickly down the bumpy garden path to the old iron gate where Mr Trevellick put out his hand and touched the lock through the ivy leaves. Then he took out the notebook which had BURTONS THE BEST BUTCHERS stamped on the cover, made some more little birds foot squiggles and underlined them.

"*Housing*," he said. "Now where shall we start? I should like to see some of these upright flats of which you spoke."

"Oh glory!" said Marcus, who felt rather like a chauffeur who had just been told to drive somewhere and who didn't know the way. He looked hopefully at Kate who was trying to catch a glimpse of the Triangle through the ivy leaves.

"If I were you," said Kate, "and you really can use the garden like a bus or a train or a taxi, I should just ask to go to the top of the highest block of flats in London."

"Very well," said Mr Trevellick meekly. He murmured something which sounded rather like Latin to Marcus and Kate, and then lifted the leaves like a curtain, pushed open the gate, and walked through it. Kate went next, almost stepping on his heels, but Marcus paused and as he did so he had the strangest feeling. He was halfway through the gate into the Triangle because Kate had hold of his sleeve, but one of his feet was still in the soggy grey garden of Wandle Heights. Before him he could see what looked like some misty iron girders and planks of wood and a clear light blue sky, but as he turned his head he also saw the backs of the houses and the stunted little apple tree in the middle of the lawn, but they were all shadowy and blurred.

"Oh come on, do," said Kate's voice from a long way off and then there was a tug on his sleeve and he was pulled through the gap after the others, and at once Wandle Heights disappeared and he found himself perched on some scaffolding with Kate, very white in the face, by his side.

"It was horrid," she said shakily. "You went all misty as though you were melting away."

"You were the one who vanished," said Marcus crossly and then he added in quite a different voice, "Oh crikey!"

All three of them were standing on a very small wooden platform which luckily had an iron railing running round it. Beyond that there was nothing but sky, while far, far below was London. Marcus who had never cared for heights and who didn't even much like climbing the ropes in the gymn at school, felt quite sick. But Kate was delighted by her bird's-eye view and was looking down at the tiny streets and rooftops with a happy smile. She climbed onto the railing and perched on the edge. Marcus shut his eyes and grabbed at the skirt of her raincoat.

"Don't do that," said Kate. "You almost made me overbalance. Oh look, there's the Thames and St Paul's and Nelson's Column and Battersea Power Station and that odd building over there must be the GPO Tower. I've seen a picture of it in the newspapers."

"What is GPO?" said Mr Trevellick, scribbling away in his notebook.

"General Post Office," said Marcus who still had his eyes tightly shut. "We must have made an awful mistake. This isn't a flat."

"It's going to be," said Kate, leaning over further than ever. "Don't you see, we said the highest flats and so they are, but they're not all built yet. Oh what fun."

"How are we going to get back?" asked Marcus. He would have given a year's pocket money at that moment to be in the nice dull ordinary garden at Wandle Heights.

"The Garden only works one way, of course," said Mr Trevellick, "so I suppose we shall have to climb down. This really is a remarkable piece of building and I wouldn't have believed it possible if I hadn't seen it with my own eyes. But how tired the people must be when they finally reach the top——and lonely too, I should have thought."

"Why lonely?" said Marcus, who was trying not to think of how they could possibly get back to nice solid ground again.

"So far away from everything," replied Mr Trevellick swinging his arms in a great circle. "Like a bird at the top of a tree. Only they have wings."

"I wish we had," said Marcus with deep feeling.

"Never mind," said Kate, climbing down from her perch. "There's a ladder at the side."

"I'll go first," said Mr Trevellick who had now noticed Marcus' pale face and set expression. "You follow me, and Kate can come last."

The wind whistled through the boards and sang round the girders which seemed to sway slightly. A tiny toy tug, hundreds of feet below on the thin little grey ribbon which was the Thames, hooted shrilly and a flock of starlings swept past on their way to Trafalgar Square. Mr Trevellick slowly began to descend the ladder which led to the platform below. It seemed to be a very long climb to Marcus, but he clamped his teeth together and concentrated on what he was doing until he heard Kate's voice say, "There's a staircase here, that'll make things easier."

Marcus leant against the wall and tried to stop his knees from trembling while Kate dusted off some of the dirt from her raincoat. They were standing on a proper concrete floor now, with walls round them, and Mr Trevellick with Kate at his heels went round exploring all the rooms.

"I should think this'd be a bedroom," said Kate. "And

the kitchen here, and this is the bathroom, of course and . . ."

"Please, please, I can't write so fast, How many people would live in a flat like this?"

"Flat. Oh, about one family. A mother and a father and two children."

"Where do the children play?"

"Anywhere, I suppose," Kate said doubtfully. "I don't think I should like it, always having to be indoors."

All the rooms had that rather sad neglected feeling about them that you find in empty buildings and Kate felt quite glad when Mr Trevellick finally said that he'd taken enough notes.

"It's a lovely view anyway," said Kate propping her elbows on the concrete window-sill and looking out over London. The buildings seemed to go on for ever, wave after wave of them, from the hills of Highgate to the rolling slopes of Wimbledon. The creeping red buses and the lines of cars looked small enough to pick up, while the people were only tiny black dots.

Marcus led the way down the staircase, his shoes as usual making a great deal of clatter. So much so, in fact, that a man in dusty blue overalls and a flat cap came out of a small wooden hut down by the front entrance and shouted:

"Who's that?"

Mr Trevellick, Kate and Marcus all stopped still and bunched together in a nervous group. The man came stamping into the entrance hall and then stopped short when he saw them.

"And what may you be doing?" he asked.

"We were looking at the flat," Mr Trevellick replied.

"Oh were you indeed! Trespassing that's what you were doing."

"Trespassing?" said Mr Trevellick with interest and wrote the word in his notebook. "If that was wrong then I'm sorry. You see I have to make a report on housing conditions and my two young friends were helping me."

"Don't," whispered Kate. "Don't tell him, he'll never believe us." But the man stopped looking annoyed and smiled instead.

"Oh I see, sir," he said, "Well, that's different then. Is there anything else you'd like to inspect? Have you seen the demonstration flat?"

"I don't think so," Mr Trevellick said cautiously.

"Half a jiff and I'll get my keys," the man said and hurried back into his little hut to reappear a moment later with a jangling bunch in his hands, "Mind you," he said as he led the way across the muddy compound, "I wish they'd let me know when you inspectors are coming round. No offence of course but it would make things easier for me. All the men are off having their tea. This way, sir."

"He thinks Mr Trevellick's from the Council or something," whispered Marcus, who felt much more his old self now that his feet were back safely on the ground.

The man marched through the echoing entrance hall and opened a brightly painted blue front door.

"The demonstration flat," he announced, "All mod cons."

"Mod who?" asked Mr Trevellick, but luckily the man didn't hear him and Marcus was able to make Mr Trevellick keep quiet by shaking his head and frowning.

"I won't stay," the man said, "as I've got some work to get on with. If you'd kindly return the keys to me when you've finished, that'll be fine, sir."

"Certainly," said Mr Trevellick politely. The front door shut with a click and the three of them began to look round. The flat was beautifully furnished with bright carpets and curtains and shiny tables and chairs, and there were some china geese hung on the walls which especially took Kate's fancy.

"Oh my," said Mr Trevellick bouncing up and down on the fat sofa. "How very beautiful it all is, and how clean and tidy."

"That's because nobody lives in it yet," Marcus replied. He wandered into the kitchen which was quite different from the one at Wandle Heights because it was full of white and gleaming machines.

"And what is that?" asked Mr Trevellick coming up behind him.

"A mixer I think," Marcus said and pressed a button. Immediately the little machine began to hum quietly to itself as it spun round and round.

"Let me, let me," implored Mr Trevellick. "Horace showed me how to work the electric light switches and the fire of gas, but this is much more fun."

He began to skip round the room turning on all the gadgets he could find and soon everything from the washing machine to the cooking stove was humming, churning or turning.

"This is a spit," Mr Trevellick exclaimed. "We have them too, of course, but then it takes two boys to turn them and we cook a whole ox at a time."

"You couldn't get an ox on that," said Marcus laughing. "And anyway I don't think people eat oxes any more."

"Yes, they do, ox tail," said Kate who had been exploring the bedrooms.

"If they only cook the tail, what happens to the rest of the beast?" asked Mr Trevellick, but nobody could answer that question. At the end of half-an-hour they had thoroughly examined everything and several pages of Mr Trevellick's notebook had been filled up. Everyone was beginning to feel rather tired by this time and they were just about to leave when there was a roaring noise outside.

"What's that?" whispered Mr Trevellick.

"A concrete mixer. The men have come back from their tea," replied Marcus from the window.

"Noise, noise, noise," murmured Mr Trevellick, and no sooner had he spoken than two electric drills began to work as well. He put his hands over his ears and Kate went round and switched off all the gadgets while Marcus opened the front door.

They led Mr Trevellick, who was beginning to look quite ill, across the muddy ground to the hut where the man hastily covered up the sporting page of the daily paper he had been reading and took back the keys.

"Everything to your satisfaction, sir?" he said loudly. Mr Trevellick nodded and then almost ran across to the main gates while the man looked after him with a slightly surprised expression.

"He doesn't like the noise," Marcus shouted.

"Noise?" the man said. "What noise? Oh that! You soon get used to *that*. What department does he come from?"

Kate looked at Marcus who said the first thing that came into his head.

"M.A.T."

The man nodded and wrote down the initials as though he understood exactly what they meant and the children ran quickly after Mr Trevellick who was leaning against the wire netting mopping his forehead.

"What terrible machines," he said. They watched the huge drills jumping up and down and the concrete mixer spilling out its great grey flood. "They'll never believe me. Never," he added.

"Do you think that's enough about houses and flats now?" asked Marcus as they began to walk along the pavement.

"More than enough," Mr Trevellick said firmly. "Let us go home immediately."

"I suppose we'd better catch a bus," said Marcus looking round. He coughed rather shyly. "I'm awfully sorry, Mr Trevellick, but I never thought of bringing any money with me, so if you could pay our fares we'll pay you back when we get to Miss Button's."

"Money!" exclaimed Mr Trevellick. "I don't believe I

have any either." He turned out all his pockets, but there was nothing there at all.

"Oh dear," said Kate. "It must be miles and miles to walk."

"Perhaps we could try barter," suggested Mr Trevellick. "We always use it."

"I'd like to see the bus conductor's face if we offered him our gloves and handkerchiefs for the fare to Wandle Heights," said Marcus starting to laugh. In spite of feeling weary Kate had to laugh too and even Mr Trevellick smiled, though in a puzzled sort of way.

"Well if you are sure that won't work," he said, "we must find another garden. There may be one somewhere round here. Hold on a jiff. That's rather good isn't it? I learnt it from the Key Man."

He pulled a piece of stiff yellow coloured paper out of his pocket and stared at it for a moment and then put back his head and sniffed the air.

"Can you smell magic gardens?" Kate asked curiously.

"In a way, in a way," Mr Trevellick replied. "Come."

He started off at a brisk pace and the children had to hurry to keep up with him. He had no idea about traffic, and after a few minutes during which he twice stepped off the pavement and on to the road, to the great irritation of passing drivers, Kate decided it would be safer to hold his hand.

"How exciting," she said breathlessly, dragging him away from a particularly busy crossing, "to find another garden."

"I think he's got it all wrong," said Marcus in a low

voice. "I recognise this bit of London because Daddy took me to a theatre round here once and we had tea afterwards at that café on the corner."

"Was it a nice tea?" Kate asked.

"Yes, smashing. He let me have cheese on toast and three slices of chocolate cake and ginger-beer. I was sick in the train going back to school but it was worth it. All the same I'm sure there aren't any gardens. Supposing it's one of the ones that have been built over and we have to go into somebody's house or office. They'd think we were mad."

"If we suddenly disappeared while they were talking to us, they'd think that they were the mad ones," Kate replied cheerfully. "Oh look, we're at Trafalgar Square."

They stood on the edge of the pavement and stared up at Nelson standing on the top of his very high column with the pigeons circling round him as he looks down Whitehall. The four massive lions were crouched at the foot of the column, and dozens of people, in spite of the cold nip in the air, were standing about feeding the birds.

"There," said Mr Trevellick triumphantly.

"That's not a garden," Marcus said.

"It was once, according to my map, and a very pretty one too," said Mr Trevellick lunging into the road in his excitement.

Luckily the traffic lights chose the moment to turn red and with Kate hanging firmly onto his hand Mr Trevellick strode across. They clattered down the steps and no sooner had they reached level ground than every pigeon in the place, and there were a great many of them, suddenly stopped what it was doing and began to surge towards them.

It was as if Mr Trevellick was a magnet and the birds were pieces of steel. In a great flood they waddled and fluttered across the square until they were pecking and cooing and pushing at each other in a shifting grey and brown circle at Mr Trevellick's feet.

"Well," he said proudly, "isn't that nice?"

"Why are they doing it?" asked Marcus, trying to brush a pigeon off his shoulder. It fluttered away and then came back and perched right by his ear, cooing and gobbling and pluming its feathers.

"They recognise me——for what I am, a great lover of wild life," Mr Trevellick replied. "Sometimes when I've finished work for the day I go out into the woods or onto the cliffs and talk to them for hours. They travel such a lot and see so much that they can often give one a great deal of information. I remember once . . ."

"Yes," Marcus interrupted, "But please, I really think we ought to go. Everybody's staring at us."

Not only the people who had been feeding the birds, but quite a few others as well had now stopped to watch Mr Trevellick who was covered in pigeons from head to foot. There were curious faces pressed to the windows of the red buses as they moved slowly through the traffic and Marcus could see over the heads of those standing near them the top of a policeman's helmet moving purposefully in their direction.

"Oh very well," said Mr Trevellick, quite crossly for

him. "And just when I was starting to have an intelligent conversation too. Here, hold my hands."

The children did as they were told and as they did so they had a curious swimming feeling in their heads and Marcus quite distinctly saw the startled expression on the face of the policeman before he disappeared into a grey mist. The roar of the traffic and the people's voices died away and so did the gobble and coo of the pigeons. Something cold and damp patted Kate's cheek and she put up her hand to brush it away thinking that it was yet another inquisitive bird and discovered that it was an ivy leaf.

"We're back," Kate said.

They looked round the peaceful garden at the back of Wandle Heights and saw that they were standing by the gate into the Triangle. It was as though they had never moved away from it all.

"I suppose we *did* go into the middle of London," Kate said doubtfully.

"I know we did," Marcus said, brushing three grey feathers off his shoulders. "Come on, Mr Trevellick, it must be lunch-time and I'm starving. I tell you what, I vote that we give magic a rest for a bit after this. It's a lot more tiring than I thought it would be."

"I agree," said Kate.

Mr Trevellick didn't reply and neither Marcus nor Kate noticed the rather guilty look on his face as he followed them up the bumpy garden path to the scullery door.

5. Mr Trevellick sees an Old Friend

EVERYONE felt in need of a rest after the journey to the flats, for as Marcus very rightly said to Kate, magic is very tiring especially when you're not used to it. Mr Trevellick retired to the peace and quiet of his own bedroom and stayed there for several days, writing pages and pages of notes until the pencil Marcus had lent him was worn down to a small stub which made his hand get cramp. Kate and Marcus explored the Common and went for slow rather silent walks with Mr Snip.

"Have you noticed something odd about the birds recently?" he asked one cold fine afternoon when they were on their way home.

"No. What?" asked Marcus.

"Young people these days never do notice things," said Mr Snip. "When I was a boy we were taught to use our eyes." He looked sideways at the children to see how they would take this remark, but they were getting used to his conversation by this time so, rather to his disappointment, they didn't say anything.

"Well there are a lot more pigeons about than usual," said Mr Snip shortly. "Greedy fat things. If I had my way I'd shoot the lot."

This did rouse Kate and the rest of the walk home was rather more noisy than usual. However, after tea Mr Snip taught them to play a game called Racing Demon which they very much enjoyed and peace was restored.

"And how long is your father going to be away?" asked Mr Snip as they cleared away the cards for Miss Button to lay the supper.

"We don't know," said Kate sighing. "His firm sends him all over the world and sometimes it's for months and months."

"He brings us back jolly nice presents," said Marcus, who didn't want Mr Snip to think that they were feeling sorry for themselves. "He's in Istanbul at the moment."

"I was married once," Mr Snip said suddenly. "But we never had any children and then my wife died. Oh well, it's all a long time ago. You'd better get out the mats, Kate. Come along, girl, come along."

"Perhaps he's lonely and that's what makes him so cross," Kate said later when she and Marcus were going to bed. "I say, wouldn't it be splendid if he married Mrs Button?"

"Now don't you go suggesting anything like that," Marcus said in alarm.

"Psst." Mr Trevellick's anxious face appeared over the banisters. "Could you manage tomorrow? I've finished my report on Housing."

"All right," Marcus agreed, "as long as we don't have to go to the top of any more buildings."

"Oh no." Mr Trevellick shook his head. "This time it's Transport."

"Well anyway," said Kate padding into the bathroom to turn on the water, "even Mr Trevellick won't be able to do much wrong riding on a bus."

"I wouldn't bet on it," said Marcus. But Kate didn't hear because of the noise the water tank was making, so he went back to his own room and wrote a long airmail letter to his father until it was his turn to have the bathroom.

This time both children remembered to take some money, and soon after breakfast on the following morning they went to stand at the bus stop on the edge of the Common.

"I'll pay the fares," Marcus said firmly as the bus drew up. Mr Trevellick took a deep breath and stepped on board and Kate pushed him up the stairs to the top deck.

"Oh dear," said Mr Trevellick as the bus started off. "It goes very fast doesn't it?"

"There's nothing to be afraid of, honestly," said Kate.

"I am not in the least afraid," Mr Trevellick replied coldly. The bus chose that moment to turn a corner and he gave a little moan and shut his eyes.

"What's the matter with your friend?" asked the Conductor.

"He's not very good at travelling," replied Kate.

"Ah, one of those," the Conductor said nodding his head. "My dad was a bit like that. He used to walk everywhere, even when he was past seventy he thought nothing of a ten mile stroll. Give me the buses every day though. Where to?"

"Clapham Junction please," said Marcus, who had thoroughly enjoyed working out a route for them to follow.

"One four and two twos," said the Conductor reeling the tickets out of the little machine which was slung round his neck. "Cheer up, sir. You'll soon be there."

He rolled away again, whistling to himself, and Kate said, "What a nice man."

"Most considerate," agreed Mr Trevellick who had now plucked up enough courage to look where they were going. They had left the Common behind and were trundling over the railway bridge and down a hill. There was more traffic now and Mr Trevellick watched a motor cyclist weaving in and out of the cars with round-eyed astonishment. He tried to write something in his notebook, but the movement of the bus made it too difficult so he had to stop.

"This is the Junction," said Marcus as they slowed down. "Kate you go in front of him and I'll go behind. Just in case you know," and he winked. They crossed the main road at the traffic lights and then went up the little alleyway which led to the station. To get to the booking office they had to go underneath the railway itself and Mr Trevellick jumped nervously as a train roared past just above their heads.

There were very few people standing on the platforms and Marcus would have liked to have gone right out to the end to watch the trains go past. There were dozens of them, from small electric suburban trains with four carriages to the mighty diesels with their mournful whistles and the great steam engines which made everything shake as they thundered past.

"Like dragons," whispered Mr Trevellick, clutching Kate's hand for comfort.

"Yes, I daresay," agreed Kate, who had never, of course, seen a dragon, but who wanted to be kind. "But you know dragons want to hurt you——at least I suppose they do——but trains wouldn't do that. They keep on their rails."

"They'd hurt you if you got in their way," Mr Trevellick pointed out, and shivered.

"The next train is for Waterloo; Waterloo only," said a voice over the loudspeaker.

It glided in and Mr Trevellick, who was now quite pale round the mouth, was dragged into an empty carriage by Marcus.

"You must think me a terrible coward," he said as they moved forwards. "It is just that everything is so strange to me. When I first started as an apprentice magician I had to spend a whole night alone in Odin's Wood and I thought that was bad enough, but this is far, far worse."

"I suppose it's all a matter of what you're used to," Marcus said thoughtfully.

"Where is Odin's Wood?" asked Kate.

"Between Tintagel and Tristram's Rock," replied Mr Trevellick. "As it turned out it was really quite peaceful. There were a few wolves about of course, but I lit a fire so they kept their distance. I never realised until now how peaceful my own time is. Even my uncle's workshop is going to seem quiet after this."

"What does he do?" asked Kate.

"He's the blacksmith and a very fine craftsman. Foreigners come from as far away as ten miles for him to shoe their horses," said Mr Trevellick proudly.

A train going in the opposite direction pounded past at this moment and the sudden rush and roar made even Kate and Marcus jump. Mr Trevellick threw himself face down on the floor and covered his ears with his hands.

"I do hope he doesn't do that in the middle of Waterloo," whispered Kate as Marcus knelt down and patted Mr Trevellick's shoulder.

The train slowly drew into the great station and once

they had dusted down their friend's thick and bulky coat and assured him that: No they really didn't think he was being very cowardly, and: Yes they really did understand how he felt, they managed to get him out onto the platform. They went through the barrier and Marcus suggested that they should go and have a quiet cup of tea in the refreshment room.

Mr Trevellick sat at a corner table and wrote up his notes with a shaky hand while Marcus did the best he could to answer all his questions. He had always thought, up till now, that he knew quite a lot about trains, but Mr Trevellick was extremely thorough and finally Kate had to go and get a whole lot of free pamphlets from a little office. Once Mr Trevellick got the hang of how a timetable worked he was delighted with it, and Marcus nudged Kate's foot under the table and whispered, "Do you think we dare risk the Underground?"

"I don't know," replied Kate, frowning almost as much as Mr Trevellick usually did. "It's worse than taking a little child round with you."

"The Underground?" asked Mr Trevellick, carefully folding up all his papers and putting them in the leather pouch he had strapped round his waist. "What is that?"

"It's——it's trains under the ground," Marcus said.

Mr Trevellick's eyebrows rose in polite disbelief.

"Come on, we'll show you," said Marcus.

"Oh dear," Kate said under her breath.

They followed the signs which led the way to the Underground station and Mr Trevellick stopped looking a little amused at Marcus' description and started to crack his fingers instead. When they reached the escalator he had to be pushed onto it and as they slid downwards he suddenly broke away from Marcus' restraining grip and turned round and started to run upwards.

"Come back," shouted Marcus, making a grab for Mr Trevellick's swinging coat tails.

"Now then, now then, mind out, mister," said a fat woman who was trying to come down.

"Oh please, please," panted Mr Trevellick, "Let me out."

"I can't bear it, I can't," wailed Kate, who hated scenes.

"You can't go up; you've got to go down," panted Marcus who now had hold of Mr Trevellick's arm.

They struggled to and fro while the fat woman stared at them in bewildered astonishment. Then suddenly they were at the bottom and were pushed onto firm ground again. Mr Trevellick leant against the wall breathing deeply and the fat woman shoved her way past him muttering very rudely about people who ought not to be allowed out on their own.

"I shall recover in a moment," said Mr Trevellick, "A flight of stairs that moves by itself! They'll never believe that. *Never.*"

"Now listen," said Marcus, "We'll go one stop on the train. It won't hurt you and you'll be quite, quite safe with us. Only please, please, don't try and run away because there are all sorts of tunnels and staircases——"

"Moving ones?" whispered Mr Trevellick.

"Well some of them. And you could easily get lost, and then there would be the most terrible trouble."

"Lead on," said Mr Trevellick bravely. "Whatever is to come, it can be no worse than that fiery monster who flew past us before."

"It was only another train," said Marcus, who already felt quite tired and shaky himself. "Now Mr Trevellick, just hold tight."

They took both his hands and led him through the little round-topped tunnels, following the lights which showed them the way to go to Charing Cross. A blast of warm air touched their already hot faces as they walked down the steps onto the platform and Kate had to hold on to her school beret to stop it blowing away. The fat woman who had been standing nearby moved away hurriedly when she saw them, and Kate pretended not to notice. There was a distant roaring and Mr Trevellick started to shiver and shake, but the children held on to him firmly and although he went alarmingly stiff, he stood his ground as the winking red eyes of the train appeared in the mouth of the tunnel and then its long red body wound its way alongside the platform. The doors slid open and Mr Trevellick was bundled inside.

The doors hissed shut and the train moved forwards. All the platform lights turned into a blur and then disappeared altogether, and then they were roaring and rattling through the darkness. Kate looked at the window opposite and saw a pale reflection of the three of them staring back at her. Mr Trevellick's mouth was wide open and his curious haircut appeared to be standing on end.

"It won't be long, it won't be long," Kate said, over

and over again. A man reading a newspaper looked over the top of it, watched them for a moment and then got up and moved hurriedly down to the other end of the carriage.

The train slackened speed, lights appeared and there were three heavy sighs of relief as they came to a halt and the doors hissed open. By the time they had reached ground level Mr Trevellick still hadn't spoken, so they walked him slowly out of the station and along the pavement to the traffic lights. They waited until the road was clear and then crossed over to the Embankment where the river Thames was lapping softly against the stone walls. A little red and blue tug bounced past on the choppy tide and a whole string of barges wallowed at anchor.

"I suppose we'd be just the same if we went back to his time," said Kate, speaking past the silent Mr Trevellick to Marcus.

"Worse probably. I'd be scared stiff if I met any wolves."

"Wolves," said Mr Trevellick, suddenly coming out of his trance, "are at least creatures of nature. Your world is full of machines. They come at you from all sides. They pick you up and they hurtle you through space. They carry you up and down. They roar, they buzz, they whir, they clank, they——"

"Look at the river. That's nice and quiet," said Marcus.

"It's dirty" said Mr Trevellick crushingly.

He had had a whole series of frightening experiences, one after the other, and he felt tired and cross. As the children felt very much the same an angry silence descended until they reached the end of the Embankment by Westminster Bridge. Big Ben boomed out that it was twelve-thirty and Marcus, who had thoughtfully borrowed a route map from Mr Snip, spread it out to find where they could catch a bus for home.

"I'm sorry," said Mr Trevellick in a small voice.

"It doesn't matter," said Kate in the kind of tone that made it quite plain that it did.

"We can get our bus over there——" began Marcus, when Mr Trevellick suddenly clapped his hands together.

"Oh, look!" he said.

"Where?" asked Kate.

"There! There!" he said pointing.

"It's only a statue," said Kate, "a statue of some old lady."

"*Some old lady!*" said Mr Trevellick in a horrified voice. "Why that's the great Boadicea, Queen of the Icinii, one of our most important Royal Personages. Oh, you don't know what it's like to see a familiar face, to recognize someone who must understand exactly how I feel in this strange world of yours."

Several people had stopped to hear these words, for Mr Trevellick was speaking very loudly and throwing his arms about.

"You promised to behave! You promised," hissed Kate.

"Oh Boadicea, Great Boadicea, hear me," called Mr Trevellick holding both hands up to the enormous statue of the Queen in her chariot.

"If you don't behave we'll leave you here on your own. I mean it," said Marcus furiously.

"Now then, now then," said a policeman pushing his way through the little semi-circle of interested people who were watching Mr Trevellick. "What's going on here?"

"It's the law," Marcus said furiously. "They'll come and take you away and put you in a deep dark dungeon and you'll never be able to get back to your own time—— I mean home again."

"And just *what* are you playing at, sir?" asked the policeman putting a friendly but firm hand on Mr Trevellick's shoulder.

6. The Birds

THE taxi ground its way through Clapham Junction with
Marcus and Kate anxiously watching the meter while
Mr Trevellick sat slumped in a corner with his hands over
his eyes. Nobody had spoken since the policeman had

got rid of the crowd, stopped a passing taxi, bundled the three of them into it and then with a horrified expression waved away the small gold coin which Mr Trevellick had tried to press into his hand.

"I was only trying to express my gratitude," Mr Trevellick said in a muffled voice as they drove over the railway bridge.

"We never, never, NEVER give money to policemen," said Marcus.

"Never!" said Mr Trevellick. "Your world is full of 'nevers'. You never go up a staircase which is going down. You never have time to stop and talk to the birds. You never throw bones over your shoulders. You never..."

"It's no good," said Marcus hopelessly, "If you don't understand, you just don't, and that's that."

"I almost wish I'd never won that Travelling Scholarship," said Mr Trevellick dispiritedly.

"So do..." began Marcus and then stopped himself just in time.

The taxi, which had been going slower and slower, now came to a halt and the driver opened up the little glass panel and said, "I can't go no further. You'll have to get out here."

"Why?" asked Marcus.

"Because of the birds," the driver said. "Look at them. *Thousands* of them! I've never seen anything like it."

The others looked and saw that it was perfectly true. The roads and the pavements, the Common and the roof tops, were covered with pigeons. Like a great sea of moving grey, fawn and white feathers, they were perched wherever there was room for them.

"*Mr Trevellick!*" Kate and Marcus said in one voice. Mr Trevellick opened the door and stumbled out and immediately all the birds began to move towards him like a flood tide. Pecking, cooing, squabbling, arching their necks and fluttering their wings, they surged around him until he nearly disappeared from view.

"Will you look at *that!*" said the taxi-driver unnecessarily. "I've never seen anything like it in all my born days. Straight up I haven't."

"Pay him," said Marcus putting his last ten shilling note into Kate's trembling hand. Then very bravely he began to push his way through the birds to Mr Trevellick, who was smiling and nodding and talking in a soft cooing voice so that he sounded exactly like a pigeon himself.

"Tell them to go," Marcus ordered.

"I *won't*," said Mr Trevellick. "They're my friends. They told me that your people had been putting all kinds of horrible things over the roofs and ledges in Trafalgar Square to try to frighten them away, so I invited them to come out here where it is quieter and more friendly."

"Tell them to go," Marcus said again, so loudly that several of the birds took to their wings and whirled round his head with little cries.

"I won't, I won't, *I won't!*" said Mr Trevellick.

"You must," shouted Marcus. "If you don't I'll never speak to you again and I'll tell everyone who you are. I'll tell them about Horace and the Triangle and——and ——Ancient Britain and MAT and EVERYTHING."

"What's he on about?" asked the taxi driver, who was trying to get two birds out of his cab where they had settled for warmth.

"He's trying to get rid of the birds," said Kate, who was almost in tears with worry and exhaustion.

"You wouldn't betray me?" Mr Trevellick exclaimed in horror.

"Oh yes I would," Marcus replied.

Mr Trevellick stared at him aghast for a moment, then turned his back and began to talk rapidly to the birds. They rose in a great wheeling mass of whirring wings, circled overhead twice and then began to flap higher and higher in the cold grey sky until like some enormous black cloud they moved northwards.

"They'll never believe me," said the driver, sounding just like Mr Trevellick himself. "Not back at the rank they won't," and shaking his head he turned the taxi round and drove rapidly away down the now empty road. Marcus and Kate marched silent and trembling to Wandle Heights with Mr Trevellick trailing along behind them.

They were very late for lunch which made Mrs Button angry; Mr Snip was cross because Marcus had left his bus map behind in the excitement down on the Embankment, and Mr Trevellick went straight up to his room and locked the door. He opened it again two minutes later to hang a sign over the handle which said in large, uneven capitals: DO NOT DISTURB.

"Would you really have told everyone about Mr Trevellick?" asked Kate when, still pale and a little shaky, she and Marcus took refuge in her bedroom that afternoon.

"They wouldn't have believed me, even if I had," Marcus said simply.

"Poor Mr Trevellick," said Kate who had a very kind heart. "I suppose it wasn't really his fault. He's just not suited to modern times."

But Marcus refused to listen to this explanation. He picked up a rather dull book and pretended to read it. Kate sighed and got out an airmail letter and wrote to her father. She knew what Marcus was like when he made up his mind about something, and that the best thing to do was to wait a bit before trying to get him to see that perhaps Mr Trevellick wasn't really too much to blame for what had happened.

"Quarrelled with your new friend, I see," said Mr Snip somewhat gleefully at supper that night. "Mrs Button says he refuses to leave his room. She had to put a tray outside in the passage."

"I'll collect it for her," said Kate.

The plates were quite clean so obviously Mr Trevellick hadn't lost his appetite. Kate hesitated and then knocked timidly on the door.

"I've finished, I thank you," said Mr Trevellick's voice.

"It's me, Kate," said Kate.

There was no reply to this, so she sighed and picked up the tray and took it downstairs and went out to the steamy kitchen to help Miss Button with the washing up.

Mrs Button was sitting at the table with her own supper

only half eaten on her plate. The gravy had gone cold and greasy, and the chop looked like a small pale island in a dark brown sea.

"Oh it's you, dear," said Mrs Button, "That's very kind of you. Thank you."

She didn't sound like her usual brisk self at all and Kate noticed for the first time how lined and sad her face looked when she wasn't being busy. Even the white curls were not quite as neat as usual.

"Don't you feel well, Mrs Button?" Kate asked timidly.

"Just a bit tired that's all," Mrs Button said, sighing.

Miss Button came through from the scullery wearing a large apron and yellow rubber gloves.

"There, Mother," she said. "You've let your meal get all cold. Let me pop it into the oven and warm it up for you."

"Don't bother, dear," said Mrs Button. "I wasn't feeling very hungry anyway."

"It's those birds that have upset you," Miss Button said, scooping up her mother's plate. "I've a good mind to write to the Council about it."

"What birds?" Kate asked in a hollow voice.

"Do you mean to say you haven't heard?" Miss Button said, pausing in the doorway. "Oh no, of course, you were off for a walk with Mr Trevellick. Well, it was the most extraordinary thing. Apparently thousands and thousands of pigeons suddenly flew over this way. They must have come from all over London I should think."

"I've noticed that there have been rather a lot about

recently," Mrs Button said. "Mr Snip drew my attention to it. But this morning the sky turned quite black with them. Black!"

"Goodness," said Kate in a small voice.

"There was nothing *good* about it," Mrs Button said. "They perched all over this roof for one thing, *and* the gutters. Now some of the pipes have come loose and there are several broken slates in the garden."

"It all costs such a lot you see," said Miss Button from the scullery where she had begun the washing up. "Getting things repaired is ever so expensive."

"My father left me this house," Mrs Button said. "Oh, it was all very different them. He used to have the outside painted every five years, and there were two men who came to inspect the roof each spring. Father was very particular about things like that."

"I'm sorry," said Kate, not knowing quite what she was sorry about but feeling that she ought to say something.

"Times change," Mrs Button said, slowly getting to her feet. "And it's not your worry, dear. Thank you again for fetching the tray. At least Mr Trevellick hasn't lost his appetite."

Kate relayed all this news to Marcus who was sitting in front of the fire staring into the flames and thinking about what had happened that morning.

"I've written to the *Daily Post* about it," said Mr Snip, who had very sharp ears when it suited him. "I headed my letter: Mysterious Migration of Birds to Wandle Heights."

"I hope they publish it," Kate said politely.

"They won't," Mr Snip replied. "People aren't interested in things like that these days."

But he was quite wrong, for two days later his letter was in the paper and he was so pleased that he sent Marcus round to the shops to get six more copies, and then spent a happy morning cutting his letter out of each of them and reading and re-reading it to himself. All this time Mr Trevellick stayed firmly in his room and when either of the children happened to meet him on the stairs he only nodded gravely and passed silently on his way.

"He's sulking, that's what it is," said Marcus who now felt rather ashamed of the way that he'd lost his temper and threatened the magician.

"Have you noticed?" said Kate sadly. "The Triangle's disappeared. You can't see anything but those trees and the weeds and that horrid mattress. I suppose it's because we're all out of sorts with each other."

"*I* don't care," said Marcus, not very truthfully.

"Well I do," said Kate. "Oh, I do wish that there was something we could do to make everything nice again. I thought it was going to be such fun having the Triangle to explore and play in and helping Mr Trevellick and hearing all about Ancient Britain and magic and everything. But now it's all gone horrid."

"There's nothing we can do about it," said Marcus, who was still rather on his dignity.

"You're as bad as he is," said Kate unusually sharply. "I think you're *both* sulking. Well, I'm going to see if Mr Snip would like to go for a walk, so there."

She left the room and Marcus heard her run down the stairs, then there were voices in the hall and a moment later Kate re-appeared.

"It's Mr Snip," she whispered. "He wants to know if we'll go to a party with him."

"A party?" Marcus said in surprise. "Where?"

"At a house called The Haven on the other side of the Triangle. Do come. He'd be so pleased."

Rather grudgingly Marcus put on a clean shirt and rubbed the toes of his shoes on the back of his socks and brushed his hair. Kate had put on her best dress in honour of the occasion and Mr Snip looked very smart indeed, but his face wore an anxious expression.

"It won't be a very exciting 'do," he said, brushing up the ends of his moustache with the back of his hand, "but it's good of you to come. Good of you to come."

"We'd like to," said Kate.

"You're a nice child," said Mr Snip, stepping out briskly. "To tell you the truth I wasn't any too pleased when Mrs Button told me you were coming to stay for the holiday. I've never had much to do with children, you see."

"Who lives at The Haven?" asked Kate, who felt quite embarrassed at Mr Snip's unexpected compliment.

"People . . . old people . . . like me. It's what they call an Old Folks' Home."

Mr Snip paused at the corner of the street and Marcus noticed that the old man's face was very pale and that his mouth had turned right down at the corners as though something was hurting him.

"I knew I'd have to come to it," he said and it was as though he had forgotten that they were there and was talking to himself, "but I've kept shutting it out of my mind. When you're old your independence means a lot to you, but there's no place in the modern world for us. People haven't got the time or the patience to stop and help. Even crossing the road is a dangerous business these days, and in the shops they get so impatient if you can't remember for a moment what you want to buy. It's all rush, rush, rush. And then there's the money. Everything's so expensive and I can't afford to pay Mrs Button as much as I should. She's been very good about it, but she'd get more money for my room from somebody else."

Both Kate and Marcus felt very sorry for Mr Snip and they would have liked to have said something to cheer him up, but as they couldn't think of the right words they tactfully kept quiet.

"Well, well," said Mr Snip with a return to his usual short-tempered manner, "I don't want you to get the idea that I'm sorry for myself. Dear me, no. I've nothing to complain of and I hear that The Haven is an excellent place. Excellent."

"I'm sure it is," Marcus said huskily.

"I——" said Mr Snip and then took out a large white handkerchief and blew his nose very loudly. "I'd just like your opinion of it. Keep your eyes and ears open and report to me if there's anything you think I should know. Eh?"

"Yes, sir," said Marcus and saluted and Mr Snip gave

him a tight smile, bobbed his head a couple of times, and then led the way through a black painted gateway.

The Haven looked very like Mrs Button's house except that it was rather more smartly painted and the garden was better kept. There was a large poster in one of the front windows which read: *The Haven. Open Day. Everybody Welcome. Tea 2/6d.*

The front door was opened by a stout woman in a shiny bright blue dress who beamed at Mr Snip and shook his hand energetically.

"How do you do?" she said. "I'm Mrs Hubbard."

"Snip," said Mr Snip, and Kate had the feeling that for two pins he would have turned and run away. She had felt very much like that on the first day at her new school so she said quickly:

"And we're Kate and Marcus Dawson."

"Delighted," said Mrs Hubbard. "I believe I've seen you about. Do come in. This is open house today. Make yourselves at home."

"She seems very jolly," whispered Marcus, helping Mr Snip off with his overcoat.

"I detest jolly women," replied Mr Snip.

Luckily Mrs Hubbard was opening the door to more visitors and didn't hear, so Kate and Marcus quickly hurried Mr Snip into the front room. There were two elderly men sitting there staring into the fire and one of them rose stiffly and extended his hand.

"Colonel Jackson," he said and his voice was like the crackle of dried leaves. "I'm an inmate here," and he laughed.

"It's a very pleasant room" Mr Snip said in a rather high voice.

"Noisy," said Colonel Jackson. "It's the traffic you know. *He's* all right; he doesn't hear it, do you, Tom?"

"Eh?" said the other old man, blinking and looking up. "What's that?"

"Deaf," said Colonel Jackson nodding. "His name's Thomas Parker. "Been deaf for years. A shell went off close to him in the first World War. Well sit down, my dear sir, sit down."

He pushed forward a chair and after a moment Mr Snip did as he was told. The three old men drew close together and Kate and Marcus slipped unnoticed from the room. They made their way through to the back where two elderly ladies were sitting placidly knitting. One was very stout and wheezed as she breathed and the other was small and thin and wore a hearing-aid clamped to her chest. They looked up at the children without much interest and then went back to their work, their stiff fingers moving slowly through the thick wool.

"I can't bear it," said Kate, staring out at the neat rather dull garden.

"They're all right," said Marcus uncomfortably.

"It must be awful to be old," Kate said in a quick high voice, "I never thought about it before. But imagine not being able to hear anything for forty years and . . ."

"Fifty," Marcus corrected her.

"Fifty then, that makes it worse. And being afraid to cross the road because you can't move quickly and never having any fun or doing anything exciting. Just sitting all day."

"I expect they like it," said Marcus. "And it does look quite a nice place really."

"Oh I do *wish* we could do something lovely for them," said Kate clasping her hands together in her agitation.

The fat old lady said wheezily; "When I was young I had hair exactly the same colour as that little girl there."

"Did you dear?" said the other old lady, sighing. "When I was young my hair was so long I could sit on it. I had to brush it a hundred times a night. How it made my arms ache."

Kate tried to pretend that she hadn't heard them and she gazed intently out of the window at the brick wall at the end of the garden. Beyond that was the Triangle, grey and cold and forbidding now, and then she remembered Mr Trevellick sitting lonely and forgotten in his room.

"I wonder," said Kate, breathing heavily on the glass and screwing up her eyes as she tried to think straight.

"Wonder what?" said Marcus, who had been glancing at his watch to see if it was time for tea yet.

"I wonder if Mr Trevellick could help, really help to give everybody at The Haven a special treat," Kate said slowly.

7. Kate's Plan

MR TREVELLICK opened his bedroom door a crack and looked down at Kate's anxious flushed face. He had dark shadows under his blue eyes and he looked as if he hadn't been sleeping very well.

"Before you speak," he said hurriedly, "I wish to apologize. I have behaved very badly I know. If you have come to say that you can no longer assist me, I shall quite understand. I lost my head."

"No," said Marcus manfully. "It was my fault. I lost my temper."

"*Probitas laudatur*," said Horace, pushing his head round the side of the door. His feathers had become much sleeker and his yellow eyes were very bright, so the tonic was obviously doing him good.

Mr Trevellick winked slightly at Marcus and both of them smiled and felt much better for it. It was as though a cloud had been blown away and the sun had come out, and both of them began to apologize all over again.

Kate sat down on the bed and waited for them to finish while she thought about her plan. Horace actually allowed her to stroke his feathers while he made a little growling noise in the back of his throat like a kettle coming up to the boil.

"It is very nice to see you both again," said Mr Trevellick when he and Marcus had finally stopped saying: No, it was all my fault, really it was.

"And it's very nice seeing you," Kate said politely. "Actually we came to ask you a favour, apart from apologizing of course," she added hastily.

"I know, I know," Mr Trevellick replied, striding up and down the bedroom and nearly tripping over Marcus' feet which as usual had managed to get in the way. "Miss Button has already told me many times about the damage done to her roof by the birds. I understand that your thatchers charge a lot of money."

"Well, it isn't really thatch you know," said Kate. "It's the tiles and the gutters. Can you help her?"

"I could, of course," Mr Trevellick said, cracking his knuckles, "and I have discussed the matter thoroughly with Horace. I suggested a very simple spell which I learnt as a first year student. Within two hours the whole roof would have been beautifully repaired and all the broken gutters replaced. But Horace said no. He said Miss Button would be bound to ask a number of rather difficult questions. Such a pity. I should have enjoyed it."

Marcus caught Horace's eye and the bird slowly closed one lid.

"Well yes, it might have been a bit awkward," Marcus said letting out a small sigh of relief. "But to get back to why we're here. It wasn't about the roof, but about Mr Snip and The Haven."

"The Haven?" said Mr Trevellick looking faintly puzzled. "I'm afraid I don't quite follow, but pray proceed. Naturally I'll do what I can to assist you."

"It's Kate's idea. Go on, Katie, you tell him," said Marcus.

So Kate, clasping her hands tightly together, unfolded her plan while Mr Trevellick listened in silence and Marcus took over the stroking of Horace.

"Would it be possible?" Kate asked at last.

"I think it's within my powers," Mr Trevellick replied slowly. "Wait a jiff will you?" He unlocked the wardrobe and drew out a heavy square box made of dark leather.

Kate and Marcus both went across to watch him and were a little disappointed not to see inside anything more exciting than some small bottles, several sheets of thick writing paper covered in Mr Trevellick's bird's foot writing, and an object rather like an hour-glass.

"Ah-ha!" said Mr Trevellick picking this up and shaking it energetically. "This should do the trick I think."

"Should it?" Kate said doubtfully.

"Only for one hour," Mr Trevellick replied. "I'm not qualified enough to play about with time too much. It gets so terribly complicated you know, and it can lead to the most dreadful difficulties if you start transplanting people from one century to another."

"*You* were," said Marcus.

"Ah, but it took three senior members of MAT to do it," said Mr Trevellick. "And what's more, I don't mind telling you I found the whole business very unpleasant. Your air is quite different from ours for one thing and then there were months and months of preparations to make my clothes *and* I had to undergo a year's course in modern languages. You have a very complicated form of speech."

"Is yours quite different then?" asked Kate.

"Well, there are one or two similar words. *It* for instance, and *Earl*, and *Villa* for house, and *Thing*, though *Thing* means Government with us."

"How peculiar," said Kate. "Just imagine a Member of Parliament saying he was a Member of Thing."

"Yes, yes, I see," said Marcus, who as usual found himself in the position of dragging Kate and Mr Trevellick back to the point. "But what about The Haven?"

"I can give them back an hour of their youth," Mr Trevellick said, struggling into his shaggy overcoat, "but there is one slight danger." He paused with one arm only half in his sleeve. "We will be risking the Triangle."

"And we've never been inside it properly," Kate said in a small voice. She looked at Marcus who was frowning and biting his lip, but then he nodded his head so she went on, "But let's do it all the same."

"Very well," said Mr Trevellick and he smiled at her very kindly. "You see I must make it quite clear that I am only an apprentice. I've never worked through an enchanted garden before, so I'm not too sure if I can manage it properly. However, let us see."

Horace, who had been listening to the conversation sidled over to Marcus and gently inserted himself in the front of his raincoat.

"He doesn't like being left out of things," whispered Mr Trevellick opening the bedroom door. "Oh help, I nearly forgot my timer."

He darted back for it and then followed them down the stairs. Mrs Button was having a nap and Miss Button was still out at work so they were able to slip out to the back garden without being seen. Mr Trevellick opened the gate into the Triangle and with the others treading on his heels he led the way inside.

Both children experienced again that strange upside-down dizzy feeling that they had had before. When the ground finished shivering under their feet they opened their eyes and for the first time they were able to really look at the garden at close quarters.

"Why, it's turned quite warm," said Marcus slipping off his coat and making Horace mutter crossly to himself. The owl fluttered away and perched on the bough of a tree.

"It's lovely," said Kate. "It's the loveliest garden in the world."

"That's because it's the perfect garden for you," Mr Trevellick replied also taking off his coat and neatly folding it. He placed it on the plinth of one of the marble statues and then sat down on it and began to murmur under his breath in the language which sounded like Latin.

It was indeed very warm, for the sun was shining in a light clear blue spring sky and the grass was speckled with daisies. The little stream gurgled to itself as it splashed under the stone bridge and the statues glistened in the sunlight which filtered through the trees.

"I think I could play here forever," said Kate peeling off her shoes and socks and running backwards and forwards across the springy turf.

"It's got such marvellous trees," said Marcus who was already halfway up one. "I can see for miles and miles and there isn't a house in sight. Come on, Katie. Come and have a look."

He held out a hand and pulled her up until she was perched on the branch below him. The garden wall was still there, pink and golden in the sunlight now, but beyond that there was nothing but rolling green hills and clumps of trees and the silver ribbon of a small river down in the valley.

"That must be the Wandle," Marcus said shading his

eyes. "And this little stream runs down to join it. Gosh, Mrs Button told me that when it rains a lot the cellar at Number Four gets very wet. She said it is because of the damp course or something like that, but really it must be because the stream practically goes under her house and I suppose it floods."

"And there's the Thames," said Kate, who wasn't interested in dull, ordinary things like damp courses. "How broad it is! And there's a great marshy swamp."

"That's Battersea," said Mr Trevellick in an abstracted voice.

"How pretty everything was then," said Kate, sighing a little. "No ugly factories or big blocks of flats."

"Ah, but think of the wolves," Marcus reminded her. "I bet that at night time the only place you could be really safe was inside this garden. And there were Vikings sailing up the Wandle, don't forget. It wasn't always sunny and peaceful. I'm going up further."

Kate was quite happy to stay where she was and it wasn't until Marcus was perched high above her head that she remembered that he didn't like heights.

"Don't get giddy," she called up.

"I'm not, not in the least," Marcus shouted down. "Oh, I wish I could climb like this in the gym at school."

"Ready," said Mr Trevellick from down on the ground. He helped Kate back to earth and a moment later Marcus joined them, together with Horace who had chosen to perch on top of his head.

"Now then," said Mr Trevellick, "I think I've got it all straight. Oh dear, I do hope so. It would be too awful if we all got stuck in 1910 for ever. 1910 seemed a good year, I hope you agree?"

"I don't know much about it," Kate said. "We never seem to do times like that in History. You either get stuck with the Elizabethans or the Georges, I don't know why."

"Edward the Seventh wasn't it?" Marcus asked. "And there weren't any wars were there?"

"Not here," said Mr Trevellick. "Come. I'll show you where your Haven should be, and if I were you I should reclothe yourselves."

The children hastily pulled on their shoes and socks and then followed Mr Trevellick across the warm garden to an iron gate. He took the hour-glass out of his pocket and balanced it on top of the brickwork and Marcus noticed that his hands were trembling a little.

"Now," said Mr Trevellick huskily, "you will have to get them into the garden, though I will give you what help I can. Once the first person enters through that gate I shall start the hour. Whatever happens" and his voice became stern, "they must all be out by the time the sands have run through to the bottom glass."

"What happens if somebody isn't out?" Kate asked nervously.

"I *think* they'd be stuck," Mr Trevellick replied. "But in any case it would be bound to throw everything out of gear. Are you ready?"

Marcus nodded and Mr Trevellick opened the gate for them to pass through. The moment they did so the giddy feeling returned, and then they were standing in the neat backgarden of The Haven and it was suddenly rather chilly.

"Oh dear," said Kate as the gate clanged shut behind them, "I couldn't bear it if something did go wrong and we never went into the garden again."

"It was your idea," Marcus said rather meanly.

"So there you are!" said a voice. The french windows were thrown open and Mrs Hubbard advanced towards them, "Mr Snip was becoming quite anxious about you."

"We went exploring," Marcus mumbled.

"Splendid," said Mrs Hubbard. "Such a nice little garden, isn't it? When the weather's fine my old folk come out here for an airing."

"It's quite nice now, don't you think?" said Kate and in fact the clouds did seem to have rolled away and it was much warmer than when they had first started out with Mr Snip.

"So it is, so it is," agreed Mrs Hubbard.

"I'm sure Mr Snip would like to see your garden," said Marcus loudly so that Mr Trevellick on the other side of the wall should hear them.

"Well I don't know, really," said Mrs Hubbard doubtfully and then strangely enough Mr Snip himself appeared at the windows and came bobbing down the path towards them. Behind him came Colonel Jackson and Mr Parker and the two old ladies. They moved very slowly and Mr Parker was leaning heavily on a stick while the smaller of the old ladies was being supported round the waist by the one who wheezed as she moved.

"Now then, now then," said Mrs Hubbard. "What's all this?"

"I thought I'd like to have a proper look round," said Mr Snip. Marcus went across to him and Mr Snip took his arm and leant on it rather heavily. He was smiling, but there was still a rather sad expression in his eyes.

"Tut, tut," said Mrs Hubbard. "It isn't really warm enough yet, you know, for you all to be out. Miss Prior dear, you haven't got your overshoes on."

"What does she say?" asked Miss Prior, turning up her hearing aid so that it gave out a high shrill squeal.

"Your overshoes," Mrs Hubbard repeated loudly, but neither Miss Prior nor any of the others seemed to hear her. They advanced slowly down the path to the gate where Kate was standing with her hand on the latch and her heart hammering very loudly in her chest.

"Now!" said a strained voice from inside the Triangle. "Oh dear, oh dear I do hope I've got it right."

"So do I," said Kate and turned the handle.

"Now, now, really," protested Mrs Hubbard retreating step by step as the others made for the gate, "there's nothing to see in there. It's in really a quite disgraceful state; in fact I've been meaning to write to the Council about it. You don't want to go in there, you know."

"I want to see inside it," Mr Snip said stubbornly and he pushed Marcus past Mrs Hubbard. She clasped her plump hand together and then spread them wide to try and stop them, but the old people surged past her and through the open gateway into the Triangle.

"Really!" exclaimed Mrs Hubbard in annoyance and plunged after them.

"Oh, no, not you," said Kate in distress, but it was too late. Mrs Hubbard had already squeezed herself through the gateway. "Oh I just *knew* something would go wrong," Kate exclaimed and ran after her.

Mr Trevellick closed the gate with a clang and trembling from head to foot with his exertions, leant against it.

8. The Garden Party

"You do look funny," said Marcus.

"You look pretty funny yourself," replied Kate. Marcus was dressed in a heavy tweed suit with a great many pockets and a pair of long socks, and his feet were encased in boots. Kate was wearing a starched and ruffled dress with a large sash, a bonnet with more ruffles and long woollen stockings that made her skin itch.

"I didn't know what to do about you two," said Mr Trevellick apologetically. "It was a case of your being either invisible or in period. I thought you'd prefer to be seen, otherwise . . ."

"I know," said Marcus. "Otherwise there might be more difficulties. I do feel as though I'm wearing three sets of clothes all at once though."

"I rather like mine," said Kate, twirling round and round.

"Don't do that, dear; you'll get overheated," said a reproving voice. A very pretty plump lady with sparkling grey eyes and round pink cheeks had come up beside them. She was wearing an enormous hat and a dress with a long skirt which swished over the grass, and she was carrying a very attractive parasol that was all covered in bows and lace.

"I'm sorry, Miss Bridges," Kate said and then wondered how she could possibly have known the lady's name, for she had never seen her before.

"You shall hand round the sandwiches later, dear," said Miss Bridges, giving Kate's dress a tweak and then patting her shoulder. "How warm it is to be sure."

"How pretty you look," Kate couldn't help saying.

"Thank you, dear," said Miss Bridges and the colour rose in her cheeks still more as a tall handsome young gentleman wearing a tight single-breasted suit and a high white collar——which looked very uncomfortable to

Marcus——came towards them twirling his black moustache. He swept off his straw hat and said gallantly, "Little Miss Katherine took the words straight out of my mouth, Miss Bridges. Will you give me the pleasure of walking down to the bridge with me?"

"I should be delighted, Captain Jackson," Miss Bridges said. "Katherine, Marcus, behave yourselves now."

"Yes, Miss Bridges," Kate said meekly and bobbed a small curtsy. Miss Bridges inclined her head gracefully under its sweeping hat and, laying her hand lightly on the Captain's proffered arm, she walked slowly away with him across the grass.

"Who was that?" Marcus asked Mr Trevellick, who was looking extremely warm in a knickerbocker suit.

"Why, Miss Emily Bridges, of course," Mr Trevellick replied, keeping one eye on the hour-glass whose sands were slowly slipping the time away. "The stout lady who was behind Mr Snip."

"But it can't have been," said Kate. "She was fat and old and she made a funny noise as she breathed."

"But this is 1910," Mr Trevellick said softly.

Kate stared after the plump but graceful figure of Miss Bridges who was now walking slowly beside the stream, listening to the tall man in the brown suit.

"And that's Colonel Jackson," Marcus said slowly. "I mean one day he'll be Colonel Jackson. Oh!" He thought of the young man's deep voice and powerful build, and tried to imagine him as he'd been at the Haven, when even getting up out of a chair had been an effort and his voice had been like the crackle of dried leaves.

"What's happened to Mrs Hubbard?" asked Kate.

"I'm sure you'll find her somewhere," said Mr Trevellick, his blue eyes twinkling. "Why don't you go and look before they make you start passing round the sandwiches?"

Marcus and Kate walked slowly and carefully across the grass looking at all the strange faces and trying to recognize them. All these people seemed to have an air of calm certainty about them which they had never noticed in grown-ups before. They moved slowly and their voices were full of happiness as they talked.

"I wonder if it really *was* like this," Kate said, dabbing at her hot face with a lace handkerchief which she had discovered tucked into her sleeve, "or if it's only like this because it's a magic hour."

"I don't know," said Marcus who was finding his boots not only heavy but also uncomfortable. "Do you realize that if Mrs Hubbard is less than fifty she'll have disappeared now, because she wouldn't have been born. And if she's vanished how can she come back again?"

"She'll *have* to come back, "Kate said firmly. "Even Mr Trevellick couldn't make somebody invisible forever. Perhaps she'll be a girl like me."

But there were no other children at the garden party.

Marcus and Kate walked right round the whole garden twice, growing more and more anxious.

"It's all your fault," Marcus said in a low cross voice as, very hot and sticky, they paused by the little bridge. "If you hadn't had this idea, Mrs Hubbard wouldn't have been lost."

"I tried to stop her, *really* I did," Kate said. "But she pushed past me. Supposing she's stuck somewhere between our time and this time and she never gets out?"

"It's not just that," said Marcus, fanning his red face with his straw boater. "Don't you see that when all the others go back to the present——I mean the future—— and Mrs Hubbard isn't there, there won't be anybody to run The Haven and it'll be shut down. I daresay they'll call in the police too," he added gloomily.

At this unfortunate remark Kate's face puckered up and she might well have started to cry if a very pleasant voice hadn't said gently:

"Now then, what's all this, Katie?"

Kate sniffed and turned round and found herself looking into the blue eyes of a very young man with dark hair and a small moustache.

"Come along," he said. "What's the matter? Marcus been teasing you again, the young blighter?"

Neither Marcus nor Kate could speak for a moment, for they both knew that they were looking at Mr Snip. Not the cross crotchety old Mr Snip who lived at Number Four Wandle Heights, but a jolly young man who hadn't a care in the world.

"Cat got your tongues?" he said chuckling. "That's not like you two. Marcus, old chap, you cut along and get Katie some strawberries and cream. We're not supposed to have them yet, but nobody'll see if you don't make too much fuss."

"Yes," Marcus said obediently and went off quickly with his boots thudding on the springy turf.

"Now then, now then, don't be a cry-baby," young Mr Snip said, for Kate was now thoroughly upset. When she had first had her wonderful idea, it had seemed to her that it must make everybody happy, but in a strange way seeing all the old people young again only made her feel miserable.

"I know what it is," said young Mr Snip, clicking his fingers. "It's because you wanted to go and sail your new boat on the pond today and instead you've had to come to the garden party. Never mind, there's always to-morrow."

"What pond?" said Kate still sniffing.

"What pond indeed? Now you're the one who's doing the teasing. Why the one on the Common of course, where we always go. To tell you the truth, Katie, I'd rather be there myself than togged up in all my finery."

"I thought you liked garden parties," said Kate, trying to find a safe subject, for she could foresee that there would be endless difficulties if they began talking about things outside the garden.

"Me? Never!" said young Mr Snip, "Just a jolly boring waste of time having to do the polite with everybody."

"Who's doing the polite, Snips old chap?" asked a second young man, coming up to them with a banjo under his arm. He was taller than young Mr Snip and a few years his senior. "I haven't noticed you being very gallant. There's Miss Bridges over there been trying to catch your eye for the last half-hour. Eh? What?" And he winked heavily at Kate who chuckled.

"Not she," said young Mr Snip, "and you shouldn't say things like that in front of Katie. Little pitchers have long ears. Anyway Miss Bridges is perfectly happy with that chap Jackson."

"Handsome girl," said the young man putting up a monocle and surveying the scene through it.

"Are you going to sing afterwards?" asked young Mr Snip.

"Well, I dunno. I might. I'm a bit out of practice, actually. Cheerio, for now," The young man strolled away and young Mr Snip laughed and said:

"Old Tommy's dying to sing I know. If you ask me, wild horses wouldn't stop him."

"Tommy Parker?" said Kate in a low voice.

"*Mr* Parker, to you, Katie," young Mr Snip said.

"But he's deaf," said Kate, forgetting to be careful.

"Deaf? Not him. Deaf to a few hints about lending a chap a fiver now and again perhaps, but not deaf otherwise. Whatever gave you that idea?" asked young Mr Snip and then luckily he went on before Kate could reply, "Oh good, here's young Marcus with the strawberries."

Marcus handed Kate a small blue and white dish full of fruit, and a long-handled silver spoon.

"I stopped to have some ginger pop," he said, running a finger round his tight collar. "You'd better hurry up with those, Katie. They're going to start serving teas in a moment."

Although the strawberries were quite delicious and the clotted cream was better than any Kate had ever tasted before, she didn't enjoy them. She kept looking at young Mr Snip who was leaning against a tree with his straw hat on the back of his head, whistling softly to himself. Beyond him was the pretty girl in the white dress, talking to Captain Jackson, and young Mr Parker who was making them both laugh.

A young lady with thick shining auburn hair and a line of freckles over the bridge of her nose came running up to them. Her flowered yellow hat was sliding out of position and she hastily pushed it straight and skewered it into place with two long pins.

"Drat the thing," she said. "I never can get my hats to stay on properly."

"That's because you've got such lovely hair," young Mr Snip said quietly, and something about the tone of his voice made both Kate and Marcus know instantly that he wanted to be alone with the young lady.

"Have I, Cyril?" she said softly. "Marcus dear, could you go and help with the tea? And Katie, be an angel—— somebody's brought a baby, and the nursemaid seems to have abandoned it. The poor thing's crying dreadfully."

"Yes, of course, Miss Prior," Kate said, and she went off quickly, leaving young Mr Snip talking in a low voice to the pretty birdlike girl who Kate knew with awful certainty, would one day become old Miss Prior who couldn't walk properly and who could only hear what people said through a deaf-aid machine.

"Cheer up, old thing," Marcus said thumping his sister on the back. "You look as if you've lost a shilling and found sixpence."

"I can't help it," said Kate. "And anyway it's much, much worse than that. "She left Marcus by the shining silver tea urn which had been set out on a table by the bridge. There were also plates of sandwiches, and a very rich looking fruit cake, and biscuits cut into all sorts of unusual and interesting shapes. Kate plodded on across the grass to the edge of the garden where there was a baby carriage from which were coming cries of anger.

"Hallo, baby," said Kate, sitting down on an iron garden seat and gently rocking the carriage backwards and forwards. The baby, which looked extremely hot, as well it might since it was wearing a great many frilled clothes and a frilled cap as well, subsided into red-faced silence and watched its own fat fingers trying to reach the lace on the edge of the elaborate canopy which fluttered above its head.

"It's so sad," said Kate, who was finding the rocking rather soothing herself. "They're all young and happy and handsome, but I know that they are going to grow old and stiff and deaf and that they'll think that nobody loves them any more."

"Bah, bah, bah," said the baby, blowing bubbles.

A small shape fluttered down onto the seat at Kate's side and Horace said softly:

*"*Ah. Donec virenti canities abest morosa.*"

"Yes, I daresay," said Kate who hadn't understood a word of this. "But it is dreadfully sad all the same."

She went on rocking and the baby slowly fell asleep while the shadows moved silently across the grass and a

*So long as youth is green and testy old age is far off.

faint warm wind stirred the branches of the trees. Kate slipped onto her knees and began to make a daisy chain, which she draped across the pram, and then she sat with her chin cupped in her hands and her feet dangling watching the garden party.

"*Tempus fugit*," said Horace suddenly.

"Even I know that," said Kate. "It's something about Time flying. Oh!"

She slithered to her feet and began to run across the grass to where Marcus was politely handing Miss Bridges a large slice of fruit cake.

"I really *cannot* resist it," she was saying, as Kate came up to them.

"Quite, quite, what?" agreed Captain Jackson, twirling his black moustache.

He would quite obviously have agreed with Miss Bridges at that moment if she had said that the world was flat.

"The time," Kate whispered in Marcus' warm ear.

"I can't see my watch," said Marcus and he turned his wrist round quite forgetting that he had at that moment picked up a cup of tea to hand to Miss Bridges. The steaming liquid went all over the front of her white dress and the cup fell to the ground and broke in two with a soft crack.

"Oh dear!" exclaimed Miss Bridges. "Oh Marcus, how could you?"

"I'm terribly sorry," he exclaimed making a dab at the stain with his handkerchief, on which he had unfortunately cleaned his hands after he had had some strawberries.

"Don't be a chump," said Captain Jackson. "That'll only make it worse. Allow me to escort you indoors, Emily, I mean Miss Bridges," and glowering very fiercely over his shoulder at Marcus he led Miss Bridges towards the gate. Miss Prior who had been talking softly to young Mr Snip said regretfully.

"I'd better go and help. You *are* naughty, Marcus."

"I know," he said hanging his head.

"I'll come with you," said young Mr Parker.

"And so will I," young Mr Snip said instantly.

"Really there's no need," said Miss Prior looking from one to the other of them and laughing gently.

"Allow me," said young Mr Snip, proffering his arm.

"Allow *me*," said young Mr Parker, glaring at his rival across Miss Prior's pretty face.

She took both their arms and the three of them strolled towards the gate where Mr Trevellick was standing, anxiously watching the hour-glass which now had very few grains of sand left in its top half.

Marcus started after the others and then doubled back and picked up two slices of the cake and pushed them into one of his many pockets. As he did so the air seemed to grow heavy and still so that he could hardly breathe, and the earth began to spin under his feet.

"The baby," called Mr Trevellick's voice anxiously. "Get the baby."

Kate just had time to grasp the handles of the springy baby carriage and to propel it, bouncing and jolting, across the grass. The baby woke up and began to howl, and the daisy chain was thrown out and trampled into the ground in Kate's headlong flight for the gate. Mr Trevellick was only just managing to hold it open, for it seemed to have developed a will of its own and was swinging heavily shut with a screeching sound.

"Hurry! Hurry!" panted Mr Trevellick and then, just as Kate thought that she was going to be trapped in 1910 for ever and ever, she was out of the Triangle and all she could hear was a great rushing sound in her ears. Slowly it died away and feeling rather sick, Kate opened her eyes and saw Marcus wearing his ordinary clothes and watching her with a thoroughly frightened expression on his face.

"There, there, dear," said the jolly, booming voice of Mrs. Hubbard. "I'm sorry if you're upset but there really isn't any point in going into the Triangle. It's in such a dreadful state."

Kate shook her head and stared silently at Mrs Hubbard's kindly pink face. She had never thought that she would be so pleased to see it again. At least she hadn't vanished forever, or got lost somewhere in time. And then Kate looked past the stout lady and saw the five old people walking slowly and with difficulty through the french windows and into The Haven. Mrs Hubbard hastened up to the house after them. Kate's mouth trembled and she looked beseechingly at Mr Trevellick, who put a reassuring arm round her shoulder.

"They *were* happy," he said gently. "They had a wonderful hour of their lost youth. Try not to be too upset." Kate nodded because she still couldn't speak properly and Marcus cleared his throat and said:

"But Mrs Hubbard——what happened to her?"

Mr Trevellick rattled the gate to make quite sure that it was securely shut and then picked up the hour-glass and stuffed it into his pocket.

"Didn't you recognise her?" he asked. "Why, I thought she was a remarkably fine infant."

Marcus and Kate exchanged glances, remembering the plump baby who had gurgled and blown bubbles in the high-wheeled carriage. And then, in spite of their lingering feeling of sadness, they both began to laugh as they followed Mr Trevellick up the neat garden path to the french windows.

9. Boadicea

"I REALLY don't know what's come over Mr Snip," said Mrs Button who was peeling potatoes in the kitchen with Kate and Marcus to help her. "Only this morning I heard him whistling away in the bathroom while he

shaved. Some old song it was; it took me right back to
my own girlhood."

"Perhaps something nice has happened to him," said
Marcus giving Kate the ghost of a wink.

"I wish something nice would happen to me" said Mrs
Button with a small sigh.

"How's the roof?" asked Marcus in an off-hand voice,
wondering if Mr Trevellick and Horace had been able
to work out a solution between them.

"Well, no more tiles have come off, thank goodness,
but there's a nasty leak in the waste-pipe in my bedroom.
And there's a damp patch on the wall that never used to
be there, I'm sure."

"Couldn't you sell this house?" asked Marcus.

"Chance would be a fine thing," Mrs Button replied,
sweeping all the potato peelings into a bowl and handing
it to him. "These days nobody wants to buy these large
houses except to turn them into flats. And this one would
need a great deal of money because there's so much wrong
with it, I'm afraid. Take those out to the compost heap,
will you, dear?"

Marcus walked up to the end of the garden and emptied
the potato peelings onto the small rather smelly pile
which was made up of last year's grass clippings and a few
odds and ends of kitchen waste. He looked at the back of
the house and saw that not only was there a damp patch
outside Mrs Button's window but that part of that
gutter had also come away from its moorings.

"Now that Mr Snip's cheered up," said Mrs Button
back in the kitchen, "Mr Trevellick seems down in the

dumps. He's been looking very seedy these last few days, have you noticed?"

"I expect he's been working too hard," said Kate, who knew very well that the affair of the garden party had exhausted Mr Trevellick rather more than he cared to admit.

"I know," said Mrs Button, slowly filling a large saucepan with cold water. "He's up in that room writing till all hours. I must say that I didn't care for the look of him when he first arrived, but there doesn't seem to be any harm in him really. He's just a little strange. Why only yesterday he asked me if I had any old scraps of my chair covers or carpets I could let him have. I managed to find him a few little odds and ends in my rag-bag, but when I asked him what he wanted them for he got quite red in the face and mumbled something about showing them to his mother."

"Perhaps she's going to refurnish her house and Mr Trevellick wants to help her," suggested Kate, watching the potatoes start to dance about in the water as it grew hotter.

"His family live in Cornwall, I understand," Mrs Button said, bending down stiffly and lighting the grill. "I've never been there myself but I should like to visit it one day. Thank you, dears. That's all you can do to help me at the moment."

As Kate and Marcus reached the doorway she straightened up and said:

"It's been on my mind that there isn't much for you to do here. I hope you're not too bored?"

"Not in the least. Honestly," Marcus said, smiling.

They climbed up to the top landing, knocked on Mr Trevellick's door, and went in. His table was covered in neat little scraps of material, piles of old bus tickets, a map of the underground, and sheets and sheets of his thick writing paper. Horace was perched on the mantlepiece admiring himself in the glass.

"How's your work going?" asked Marcus.

"Not too badly, I suppose," Mr Trevellick said, massaging his cramped fingers. "The difficulty is to pick out the important bits. I have written many pages about the trains which travel along the ground, also those which go underneath it." He shivered slightly as he spoke and Kate said hastily:

"What about Housing?"

"Yes, that *was* a little easier," said Mr Trevellick brightening up, "I have described the upright flats and also this house in great detail, as well as your method of joining houses together in strings. I have toyed with the idea of suggesting that we do the same thing with our huts, but then, of course, that could lead to difficulties with the animals."

"Do you mean you keep pets?" Kate asked with interest.

"Not exactly," Mr Trevellick said. Horace made a snorting sound in the back of his throat, and then shut his eyes and pretended that he had done no such thing. "We have chickens and goats and sheep and we share a cow: one cow to every three families."

"And they live in your gardens?" asked Kate.

"In the fine weather we keep them fenced in. But when it gets cold they come indoors with us naturally," Mr Trevellick replied, shuffling all his papers into one neat pile.

"I don't think that would be allowed here," Kate said regretfully. It would be very nice she decided to share a house with so many assorted animals.

"I'm sure it's against the law," said Marcus firmly.

"Ah, now that's something you have got a lot of," said Mr Trevellick. "Laws for this and laws for that. It's no wonder you have to have such a large police force."

"I'm sure your mother'll be awfully pleased with the bits of carpet," Kate said quickly as she saw Marcus looking rather annoyed at Mr Trevellick's last remark.

"I expect she'll nail them to the wall when my teachers have stopped examining them," said Mr Trevellick. "They'll be very useful for keeping out the draughts. We put rushes on the floor. It's a much better idea than carpets really, because you just throw them away when they get dirty and then put down fresh ones."

"You don't like it here much, do you? asked Marcus, going straight to the point as usual. Mr Trevellick fiddled with the large bone comb with which he had been trying to tidy his thick hair and then said in a low voice:

"It's not that, exactly. It's just that all your ways are so strange to me and I can't help feeling a bit lonely sometimes with no one of my own to talk to."

"You've got Horace," said Marcus, feeling rather hurt.

"It's not the same," Mr Trevellick said with a ghost of a sigh. "Come, let us go down to the evening meal.

There at least I have no fault to find. Mrs Button's cooking is excellent."

It was just after midnight that Marcus woke from a deep sleep to hear a familiar husky voice calling him from the window-sill. He stirred and sat up, rubbing his knuckles in his eyes.

"It's you, is it," he said to the shadowy grey patch by the curtain.

"*Pax, pax simplicitus*," Horace said croakily.

"I'm not simplicitus. What's wrong?" Marcus asked.

"Trevellick. *Festina——*" said Horace.

"It's no good," Marcus said after several puzzled seconds. "I can't remember what that means and I've left my Latin dictionary at school. I didn't think I'd need it in the holidays."

"*Festina*," Horace croaked again, moving from claw to claw.

Marcus put his hands over his ears to think better. The owl was obviously very upset, and as it didn't like children it probably wouldn't be here unless something was very wrong.

"*Hurry. Hurry*," Marcus said suddenly, "Gosh, I never thought I'd remember that bit. But why? What's Mr Trevellick up to now?"

He clambered out of bed and ran to the window where he was just in time to see a shadowy figure walking rapidly up the garden path towards the brick wall. Marcus didn't dare call out in case he roused everybody else up, so after a moment's hesitation he snatched up his

*Peace, peace, simpleton.

dressing-gown and tiptoed into Kate's room to wake her.
Horace, having merely flown along the outside wall was
already on her window-sill.

"Mr Trevellick's gone off on his own," said Marcus
as soon as Kate was awake enough to understand what
was happening. "We'll have to go after him."

"*Festina! Festina!*" urged Horace, fluffing up his
feathers and glaring at them.

"What does that mean?" Kate asked.

"Hurry," Marcus said. "And we'd better. He's
probably gone back to talk to the pigeons. You get
dressed, but for goodness sake, keep quiet."

He crept out again and put on his own clothes in the
dark, which was not at all easy, and it wasn't until long
afterwards that he discovered that he'd got his school
sweater on inside out, as well as his socks. Three minutes
later he and Kate were tip-toeing down the stairs and
across the dark silent hall.

"I feel like a burglar," whispered Kate.

"Shh," Marcus said.

As they crossed the kitchen a mouse scuttled out from
behind the old stove and made Kate jump. But with a
great effort she managed not to make a sound and then
Marcus slid back the bolts on the scullery door and they
felt the cold night air on their faces. Horace was swooping
round and round rather giddily because of the orange
street lighting which made it difficult for him to see
properly.

"I don't see what we can do," whispered Kate as they
reached the damp curtain of ivy which looked a very

strange colour in the odd light. "Supposing it's just the old ordinary Triangle?"

"Horace wouldn't have called me if we *couldn't* do something," Marcus said firmly.

He pulled aside the leaves and they looked through. There was the beautiful garden with the gleaming statues and the little tinkling stream running under the stone bridge by the fountain.

"Hold my hand," Marcus ordered, and then he pushed open the gate and slipped through the gap in the leaves, dragging Kate behind him.

"Take us to where Mr Trevellick is," Marcus said clearly and as he spoke Horace swooped out of the night sky, landing rather unsteadily on his shoulder, and gripped at Marcus' school raincoat with his sharp little claws. The garden shook and shivered and grew dark. There was a rushing sound in their ears and then Marcus heard Kate's voice saying:

"I never brought any money and we could be going anywhere!"

But the scene before them was only too familiar. By the light of the cold silver moon they recognized the sleek grey waters of the Thames in front of them, while to their right was the tall clock tower of Big Ben and next to that the Houses of Parliament. The traffic lights were blinking steadily and changing from red to yellow to green, but luckily there were no buses or taxis in sight although drawn up some yards away was a long, sleek black shape.

"A police car," said Kate. "Oh what has he done now!"

"*Cave*," croaked Horace and delicately slid down the front of Marcus' mackintosh, pushed himself inside it and nestled down against the inside-out sweater. He pushed his head out cautiously, blinked his yellow eyes and pointed with one wingtip.

"Oh dear!" said Kate.

"Oh glory!" said Marcus.

He would very much have liked to have turned round and ran away, but there was nowhere to run to and also it was quite obvious that if ever Mr Trevellick had needed a friend, it was now. He had clambered up onto the plinth of Queen Boadicea's statue and was now standing with his back to it, his arms outstretched. Vainly trying to grasp his ankles were two uniformed policemen, while the third member of the dark shiny car was wiping his forehead with the back of his head.

"Now come on down, sir," said one of the policemen. "We're not going to hurt you, are we, Fred?"

"No," said Fred, putting his peaked cap back on his head and pulling down his jacket. He advanced purposefully towards the desperate Mr Trevellick. "You'll feel better in the morning, sir. Just you come on down."

"You're going to put me in a deep dark dungeon, I know," said Mr Trevellick and Marcus almost groaned. He had said that once and Mr Trevellick had taken him at his word.

"We're never," said Fred. "A nice cosy cell more like. Come along now." He had been speaking quite calmly and politely, but as he finished he made a sudden grab at Mr Trevellick's ankle.

"Oh great Queen, mighty Boadicea, aid me," called Mr Trevellick.

"Yes, yes," said the third policeman. "I daresay she will and all——oh my!" He staggered back as he spoke and then put his hands over his eyes.

"Oh!" cried Kate and tried to hide behind Marcus.

"What's he doing? What's he doing?" whispered Marcus.

*"*Necessitas non habet legem*," replied Horace blinking sleepily.

All six of them stared up at the night sky as with a strange creaking and cracking sound the great statue stirred. The horses arched their necks and threw up their heads; Boadicea's two daughters stretched their arms, and the Queen herself dropped her hands and looked down.

"I'm dreaming," said the first policeman. "That's what it is, dreaming."

"Then I'm having the same dream," said the one called Fred, "and it's a nightmare."

Mr Trevellick politely held up his hand and Boadicea leant down, grasped it, and then jumped lightly to the ground. She was extremely large and very frightening and the three policemen backed away as she walked slowly and majestically towards them.

"Shall I slay them?" asked Boadicea calmly.

"No," said Marcus. "No, you mustn't do that. Please." And in spite of being extremely frightened he darted forward and caught at the Queen's arm. It was very cold and shiny to the touch and difficult to hold.

*Necessity knows no law.

"And who is this?" she asked in her deep powerful voice, and she picked Marcus up as though he weighed nothing at all.

"Oh it's you, is it?" said Mr Trevellick. "And what are you doing here?"

"Horace woke me up and made me come after you. Please, Queen, I mean your Majesty, please put me down."

"You will be a mighty warrior one day," said the Queen laughing, and her laughter was like the tolling of great bronze bells.

"Now look here, miss," said one of the policemen—— all three of them were now backed up against the side of Westminster Bridge with the Queen's daughters standing in front of them——"I don't know how you done it and it's all very clever I'm sure. But enough's enough and we've got our duty to do. I'll have to take your names and addresses. You first please, madam."

"He speaks like a Roman guard," said the Queen, "and you know, Trevellick, what I've always thought of *them*." She dropped Marcus lightly on the road and with slow, majestic steps advanced towards the three men from the squad car.

10. Mr Trevellick Enjoys Himself

"Now you *have* done it," Marcus said in despair. "I can remember from history lessons what Boadicea did to the Romans and if she drives her chariot over those policemen it'll be all your fault."

"*She* won't harm them," Mr Trevellick said cheerfully as he dusted down his overcoat. "In spite of all that warlike talk of hers she never did like actually killing people."

"Then why have you made her alive?" said Kate.

"It was the loneliness," Mr Trevellick said simply. "When I saw Mr Snip talking to those of his own generation and you two laughing and enjoying yourselves I suddenly felt so out of things. Lying in bed tonight I suddenly remembered dear old Boadicea up here all on *her* own, and I decided there and then to come along for a chat."

"Which was when the police arrived, I suppose," said Marcus.

"I told you that your world had too many of them," said Mr Trevellick. "I meant no harm, but they absolutely refused to listen to me and then, I am afraid I rather lost my head."

"Now what's going to happen?" asked Marcus, looking cautiously round the side of Mr Trevellick. The Great Queen was standing in front of the three policemen wagging one finger at them. The men were pressed rigidly against the parapet and all of them had their eyes tightly closed.

"Could I not just have one word with her?" Mr Trevellick said wistfully.

"Well, all right," said Marcus reluctantly. "But please, please, be quick. Those policemen are going to be furious and they really will lock us up, you know. I can't imagine what Mrs Button's going to say."

"Don't worry," said Mr Trevellick, cheering up instantly. "I'll get the Queen to tell her daughters to keep an eye on them. They always were good obedient girls. Strictly between you and me I rather think they're a little afraid of their mother."

"I don't blame them," whispered Kate as Mr Trevellick went hurrying off down the bridge with his coat billowing out behind him.

"I'd never have offered to help him," said Marcus, "if I'd known what a lot of trouble he was going to be. First there was that business of finding ourselves up on the scaffolding, and then all that mess in the underground, and then the pigeons in Trafalgar Square, not to mention asking the birds back to Wandle Heights, and now this. I ask you!"

"He did help us with Mr Snip," Kate reminded her brother. "And he has been working awfully hard, so I suppose he deserves some kind of reward."

"We'll end up in prison, you realize that I suppose?" Marcus said bitterly.

"They don't send children of our age to prison," Kate said. "Oh dear, he's bringing the Queen back with him."

Boadicea's heavy tread echoed across the quiet bridge and she really looked extremely frightening as she came towards them, twirling her long spear and with her cloak flying out behind her.

"Kate and Marcus Dawson, oh Mighty One," said Mr Trevellick loudly, and then under his breath, "Kneel, kneel; she's keen on that kind of thing."

Marcus and Kate obediently dropped on their knees

and, even as he did so, Marcus couldn't help thinking how very odd it was that at two o'clock on a cold spring morning, right underneath the clock tower of Big Ben he should be presented to a Queen from Ancient Britain by an apprentice magician of the Sixth Century A.D.

"Rise, rise," said the Queen, throwing back her cloak in a gesture that was already becoming familiar to them. "I heard from Trevellick that you have been aiding him in his quest for wisdom. Is he a good pupil?"

"He tries hard," said Marcus, unconsciously echoing what the masters at school often said about himself, and then as Mr Trevellick prodded him gently in the ribs he added hastily, "Your Majesty."

"We all try hard I hope," said the Queen rather severely. "Come, let us walk a little. It is many years since I had the opportunity to take some exercise."

She turned on her heel as she spoke and began to retrace her footsteps over the bridge, passing her daughters who were standing stiffly in front of the policemen.

"I can remember," said Boadicea, "when this river was both wider and far cleaner than this muddy stream. It used to be quite pretty in my day. Tell me, Trevellick, do you remember in your time . . ."

Kate and Marcus padded along behind the Queen, getting more and more breathless, for she walked extremely fast. Luckily there was very little traffic and when an all night bus did pass them the conductor leant out and called cheerfully:

"What-oh mate! Been to a fancy dress party have you?"

"Impudence!" said the Queen shaking her spear at him, which made the conductor laugh more than ever as he was borne away towards Lambeth.

"Nobody has any respect these days," the Queen said, putting her crown straight. "If he'd dared to speak to me like that in my own time, I'd have driven my chariot straight at him *and* enjoyed it."

"Would she?" Marcus whispered to Horace and the bird shook its downy head and winked its yellow eye.

Big Ben struck the quarter and Mr Trevellick said reluctantly, "I shall have to go, Your Majesty. I promised the children that we would not stay too long."

"It's far too late for them to be up in any case," said the Queen, looking quite kindly at Kate who was struggling to hold back a yawn. "Come, little one, I will carry you," and she bent down and picked Kate up. Her arms were very cold and hard and Kate felt most uncomfortable but she tried not to show it.

"There," said the Queen, setting her down again at the foot of her plinth, "Now you can tell your mother that the mighty Boadicea has acted as your nurse."

"My mother's dead," said Kate and for a moment there was silence except for the soft gurgle of the Thames lapping against the walls.

"Your father, then," Boadicea said. "Well, Trevellick, so we must part."

"I *have* enjoyed our meeting, Your Majesty," said Mr

Trevellick earnestly, "It's really made me feel quite refreshed, you know."

"Do you stay long in this time?" enquired the Queen.

"No. I must soon return to my own century," said Mr Trevellick with a tinge of relief in his voice.

"*Tempus fugit*," said Marcus unwisely and the Queen's face darkened as she heard the language of her conquerors.

"Well, well," said Mr Trevellick hastily, while Horace pecked Marcus' arm to keep him from saying anything else unfortunate, "we must get back home. About those——er—— guards?" and he coughed delicately.

"I'll deal with them," the Queen said, her good humour quite restored at the idea of giving the policemen some more of her mind. "Wait one moment, Trevellick."

She marched majestically across to the policemen and motioned to her daughters to go back to the plinth. They saluted, turned and ran rather heavily to the end of the bridge.

"She's a bit like a schoolmistress, isn't she" Kate whispered to Mr Trevellick.

"She always was," he replied, his eyes twinkling. "If she had lived in your times I think she would have closely resembled Mrs Hubbard."

Boadicea finished speaking and then returned to the others at the end of the bridge.

"I've ordered them to wait there for another five minutes," she said, "which will give you plenty of time to go about your business."

"*Will* they wait?" Kate asked nervously.

"Naturally," the Queen replied in some surprise.

She put out her hand and Mr Trevellick knelt to kiss it. Then she did the same to the children who followed his example. She gave her cloak one last tug and then climbed up nimbly to her chariot and smoothed down her robes. Her daughters bowed their heads to Mr Trevellick and the children, and the Queen called out impatiently:

"Hurry up, hurry up."

The horses stopped arching their necks and reared up with their front legs flying out into space. The Queen raised her spear and for a moment looked down at the three gathered below.

"I, too, enjoyed our meeting," she said in her great bell-like voice. Then she lifted her head and in a moment it was as though she had never moved at all. She was just a great and graceful statue against the dark night sky.

"Come on," said Marcus snatching at Mr Trevellick's hand and starting to pull him across the road. "That five minutes will be up soon and whatever happens we mustn't let the policemen see you."

"Yes, but where to?" asked Kate. "We haven't any money and I just can't walk home. It must be miles and miles."

"Trafalgar Square," said Marcus who had been thinking things out. "We'll use the secret garden there. Oh do come on, Mr Trevellick." He broke into a run as he spoke and the others pounded after him and didn't stop until they had turned into Whitehall.

"What will the policemen do?" asked Kate as they

began to walk rather breathlessly towards Nelson's Column.

"They won't *do* anything, I expect," replied Mr Trevellick. "Each one of them will be far too embarrassed to tell the other what he thought happened, so they'll each pretend that they got out of the car to stretch their legs and that they then had a short rest leaning over the parapet."

"Truly?" asked Kate anxiously.

"Well, would you tell your friends that you were taken prisoner by Queen Boadicea and her daughters if you were a grown-up and a policeman at that?" asked Mr Trevellick.

"No, I suppose not," Kate said doubtfully. All the same she was very relieved when at last they reached Trafalgar Square without a police car drawing up alongside them.

"Mr Trevellick," said Marcus as they joined hands in front of Nelson's Column. "Promise me that you won't go off alone like that any more."

"I promise," Mr Trevellick said solemnly. "And really I find myself in your debt yet again. If you hadn't come after me I *might* have done something quite foolish."

"What?" Kate couldn't help asking.

"Well, when your guards were being so obstructive it did cross my mind that I might call on all the statues in your great city. There appear to be a great many of them. Would you like me to do it now?"

"No, no," said Marcus clinging firmly to Mr Trevellick's hand.

"I could do it, you know," said Mr Trevellick, who had after all had a thoroughly exciting evening and was now getting rather above himself.

"*Cave, cave,*" said Horace, struggling out of Marcus' overcoat and circling round and round their heads. Three taxis came slowly down the Strand, paused at the traffic lights and then as the signals changed drove towards Admiralty Arch.

"Spoil sport!" said Mr Trevellick. "Oh, very well then. Take us back, oh garden of delights and enchantment, to Wandle Heights."

Horace flapped onto Kate's shoulder and balanced there as the lights of Trafalgar Square and the dancing water in the fountains grew faint and hazy and they caught a glimpse of strange trees and flowers and then it all vanished. There was a moment's darkness and then the Triangle came insubstantially into view, steadied up and then settled down——and it seemed as though they had always been there.

"Thank goodness!" said Marcus letting out an enormous sigh of relief.

"I think I should rather have liked to have met some of the other statues," said Kate yawning and rubbing her eyes. "Especially Nelson. We learnt about him at school because he's in the Georges."

"In the what?" said Mr Trevellick, leading the way across to the gate.

"The reign of George the Fourth, at least before he was actually the Fourth but he was pretending to be King because of his father you know," said Kate who suddenly felt extremely sleepy and who wasn't finding it easy to explain things clearly.

"Never mind about that now," said Marcus, on whom tiredness was also having its effect in that it was making him irritable. "Do come on."

They walked quietly up the garden path and let themselves in through the back door which Marcus had thoughtfully left on the latch.

"Thank goodness we're back safely," Marcus whispered as they tiptoed across the shadowy hall and up the stairs.

*"*Fortis fortuna adiuvat*," said Horace softly in his ear and Marcus after working out what he meant went quite pink with pleasure. The owl flapped away up the dark well of the stairs to the top floor and they heard the soft sweep of its wings as it flew along the passage to Mr Trevellick's bedroom.

Marcus opened the door of his own room and then halted on the threshold, for there, sitting on the bed and wearing her pink quilted dressing-gown and a great many curlers, was Miss Button.

"And what," she said, getting to her feet with a swish of her quilted skirts, "is the meaning of this? Where have you been and what *have* you been doing?"

And then to the horror of the three stunned figures in the doorway, she burst into tears.

*Fortune aids the brave.

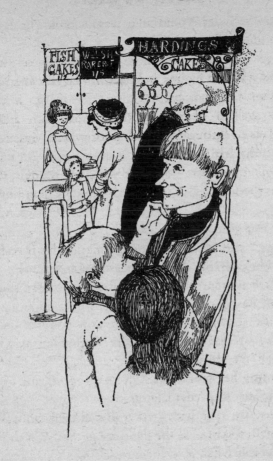

11. Mr Snip's Treat

MR TREVELLICK muttered hoarsely, "A nostrum, a nostrum," and bolted out of the room, Marcus shifted from foot to foot and looked fixedly at the floor and Kate ran across and put her arms round Miss Button's shoulders and said, "Oh don't, please don't. Please, Miss Button, don't."

"I can't go on. I can't go on," said Miss Button scrabbling in her quilted pocket for a handkerchief.

"We're quite safe and nothing's the matter with us, truly," said Kate, patting a shaking shoulder.

"It's not just you," Miss Button said indistinctly through the handkerchief. "It's everything. And I *was* so worried. I'm responsible for you and I thought you'd run away. Mother said it was dull for you here, but you seemed to take to Mr Snip and Mr Trevellick——where is Mr Trevellick by the way?"

"Gone," said Marcus, whose opinion of his friend had slipped considerably during the last few moments.

"And then there's the house falling to pieces round our ears and Mother getting older and she does find the stairs such a trial lately——her rheumatism you see——and now Mr Snip's leaving and he was *no* trouble as a lodger. Oh dear!" said Miss Button.

"Oh dear," echoed Kate.

Everything seemed to be going wrong at once, and the worst of it was that it was really all their fault. They were partly responsible for the damage to the house and it was entirely because of them that Mr Snip had become happily resigned to going into The Haven, and now they had nearly worried Miss Button to death by going off to Westminster at two o'clock in the morning.

"*A nostrum*," said Mr Trevellick, reappearing in the doorway. He was carrying his toothglass which was half-full of some bright pink liquid which smelt pleasantly of rose leaves and mint. "My very own remedy, gathered by the light of the full moon. I give it to my mother when she gets upset sometimes," Mr Trevellick said to Marcus in a low voice.

"I don't want it," said Miss Button turning her head away.

"Come along now, drink up," Mr Trevellick said firmly, just as if she were a child and not efficient bustling Miss Button at all, and he put the glass into her hand and gently lifted it to her mouth. Miss Button swallowed it down, dabbed at her face with the handkerchief and then said much more calmly:

"Really, I *do* apologize. I can't think what came over me." She straightened her back, folded her hands in her lap and went on, "Now then, please kindly explain what you have been doing."

Marcus and Kate, who had been having a rapid whispered conversation, decided to come as near to the truth as possible.

"I thought," said Marcus, "that I heard a noise, so I got up to look——in case it was burglars or something like that——and I saw Mr Trevellick walking down the garden, so I woke up Kate and we went after him."

"Walking at two o'clock in the morning," said Miss Button in an astonished voice. "Where to, may I ask?"

"To see Quee..." began Mr Trevellick and then stopped as Marcus trod gently on his foot. "It was like a dream," he went on hastily, "I hardly seemed to know where I was or what was happening."

"Oh you mean you were *sleep*-walking," Miss Button

said, her face lightening, "I see. I used to do that sometimes as a child. Once I went downstairs in my nightgown and walked straight into the dining-room where my parents were entertaining guests. Such a fright I gave them. You'd better lock your door and bolt your window in future Mr Trevellick or you may wake up one night and find yourself in the middle of London with no idea how you got there."

She laughed at this flight of fancy and the others joined in somewhat uneasily.

"Now then into bed, you two," she said briskly. "And let's have no more gallivanting about in the middle of the night. I don't think we'll mention any of this to Mother as we don't want to worry her unnecessarily, do we? Night-night."

"She did cheer up quickly," Marcus whispered to Mr Trevellick as they parted on the landing. "It must be a very good nost-whatever-you-said."

"It is," said Mr Trevellick proudly. "And night-night to you too. I've never come across that phrase before." And he crept up the stairs repeating the words over and over to himself in a soft sing-song voice.

During the following week Mr Trevellick shut himself up in his room to work, but he gave the children permission to go and explore the garden as long as Horace was there to keep an eye on them. Mrs Button shook her head over their choosing to play in that "dirty old Triangle" as she called it, but to the children, once they were through the gate, it was a garden of pure delight.

"I thought you didn't approve of us," said Marcus

as the old owl found a nice patch of shade under the weeping willow and settled down to have a quiet nap.

"Humph," said Horace and ruffled up his feathers and went to sleep.

"I'd really rather Horace stayed looking after Mr Trevellick," said Kate, kicking off her shoes and socks and dabbling her feet in the cool little stream. "But I suppose he can't get into too much trouble if he keeps in his room."

"He'll be all right," Marcus said. "After all, he did promise faithfully to behave himself. I say! Here's that cup I broke on the day of the garden party."

"What happened to the pieces of cake you picked up?" asked Kate, trying to fit the two bits of china together.

"They turned into dry dusty crumbs," Marcus replied, "I suppose a cake fifty-five years old would be like that. Pity, I never did manage to eat a proper slice of it."

"It is lovely here," Kate said, splashing her feet up and down. "If only the firm would send Daddy back from Istanbul everything would be perfect."

"Well they won't. You know he said in his last letter that he'll be out there nearly another year. Come on, let's play hide and seek. You shut your eyes and count twenty and don't cheat."

"I don't know what you do in that back garden," said Mrs Button when, tired but happy, the children returned to the house two hours later.

"We play games," Marcus said vaguely.

"We pretend that it's magic," said Kate, "and that

there's a little stream and a bridge and a weeping willow tree and some marble statues. It's wonderful fun."

"What an imagination you have got to be sure," said Mrs Button admiringly. "Marcus dear, open this tin for me, would you? I don't seem to be able to manage the opener."

"Is it your rheumatism?" Kate asked anxiously.

"Just a little perhaps," said Mrs Button rubbing her swollen knuckles. "It'll get better when the weather changes I expect. It's old age you know; it catches up with all of us sooner or later."

"We must try and think of some way to help Mrs Button," Kate said that night.

"We'll work out a plan tomorrow," Marcus replied. "And we'll have another talk with Mr Trevellick about it. If Horace is there he might be able to think of some kind of sensible magic way to do it."

But as it happened their idea of spending a quiet morning in the Triangle thinking things over, was upset by both Mr Trevellick and Mr Snip.

"Finished," said Mr Trevellick, coming down to breakfast and smiling broadly.

"What, all your work?" asked Marcus, helping himself generously to breakfast cereal.

"My reports on Housing and Transport," said Mr Trevellick. "Now all that remains is Food."

"Talking of which," said Mr Snip, coming into the room looking very smart in his best dark blue suit and his Sunday tie, "I should like to invite you to have lunch with me today. I wish to show my gratitude for your kindness in coming with me to inspect The Haven."

He said this all in one breath and Marcus guessed that the old man had been rehearsing the words to himself while he shaved, as he had heard an odd muttering in the bathroom earlier.

"Then you are definitely going to The Haven?" Kate asked after they had politely accepted the invitation.

"Yes indeed," said Mr Snip pouring out the tea. "I had my doubts about it as you know. And at first, I'll admit, I didn't take to the place too much. But as the afternoon wore on and I began talking to one or two of the inmates, as Colonel Jackson rather amusingly calls them, my doubts started to vanish. I believe I may have even dozed off for a moment or so, while you two were exploring the garden. And when I woke up I felt not only much more cheerful, but also as though I almost belonged there. It was as though I had known them all for many years. I suppose that comes from them all being of my own generation. Sugar, Mr Trevellick?"

"What? Oh yes, thank you. Three lumps," said Mr Trevellick who had been staring at Mr Snip with deep interest.

"As for that Mrs Hubbard," said Mr Snip dropping in the sugar with three splashy plops, "she's a goodhearted woman enough. Bossy, of course, but very efficient and kind——so old Jackson told me. I suppose I shouldn't really call him that, but then he is older than me, quite a few years I should think," Mr Snip added with satisfaction.

Kate thought of the dashing young captain and the

bright-eyed young Mr Snip that she and Marcus had met and talked to, and hastily sipped her tea.

"That's good then," said Mr Trevellick with a happy sigh of relief. "I am so glad for you, sir, that matters have concluded well."

"Perhaps you'd care to join our little lunch party?" said Mr Snip who was in a very sunny mood.

"I'm sure he wouldn't," and "I expect he's busy," said Kate and Marcus, both talking at the same time.

"I'd like to very much," said Mr Trevellick.

"I wasn't talking to you," Mr Snip said to the children, with a return of his old tart manner. "Very good then. We four will lunch together. I'll tell Mrs Button directly after breakfast. I daresay she'll be glad to have a rest from cooking."

"I have collected a great deal of information from the good Mrs Button as to how she prepares the meals," said Mr Trevellick when Mr Snip bustled away to the kitchen twenty minutes later. "Your system of freezing and tinning foods seems very strange to me. Also she showed me a most magical dust."

"Mrs *Button* did?" said Marcus, deciding to have a third slice of toast.

"Yes, indeed. She had this sweet-smelling powder which she emptied into boiling water and it turned into a broth. I only wish that I could take some home to my mother. She too makes an excellent broth, but she has to stew bones for many hours to do it and when the wood's damp it takes even longer."

"I don't think packets of soup cost much," said Kate.

"Yes, well," said Mr Trevellick fiddling with his teaspoon, "you see unfortunately my teachers didn't quite realize how much it costs to live in your times. Money and magic never have mixed well together you know, and they had great difficulty in providing me with any wealth at all. When they told me how much I could take with me, it seemed like a fortune, a whole twenty pounds which is the equivalent of at least two years' salary for a fully qualified magician in my century."

"Goodness!" said Marcus, who knew a boy at school who often *said* that he got that much in tips at Christmas, although Marcus had never quite believed him.

"It will exactly pay the good Mrs Button for my lodging and food, but there is nothing over," explained Mr Trevellick.

"Couldn't you magic some money," asked Kate, clearing away the breakfast things.

"You mean transmute lead into gold?" asked Mr Trevellick. "I'm not highly qualified enough to do that. Besides which, it often reverts, you know."

"I beg your pardon?" said Marcus.

"Turns back into lead again. They haven't managed to iron out that little snag yet and it can lead to awful difficulties in the case of paying out ransom money and things like that. You've no idea how it upsets some of the Earls when they go down to their cellars to count their gold blocks and find nothing but lead. I remember one particular . . ."

But unfortunately the children were never to hear this story, as Mr Snip came bustling back at this point to say

that Mrs Button now knew of all their arrangements and
was waiting to start the washing up.

As Mrs Button had decided to have a proper rest while
she was at it, she asked the children to do the shopping for
her, so they spent the morning in Wandle High Street,
with Mr Trevellick who insisted on going with them
scribbling in his little notebook. On the whole he
behaved very well, although there was one awkward
moment in the butcher's where they had been carefully
instructed to buy the best end of neck.

"What kind of neck do you suppose it means?" asked
Kate, peering at Mrs Button's rather crabbed writing
on the shopping list. But luckily the butcher seemed to
know without being told and he began to wield his
chopper with a steady thump-thump.

"I don't really like butcher's shops," said Kate, trying
not to look at the line of rabbits still in their skins which
were hanging up in a sad little row.

"It's far worse when you've lived in the same room
with an animal for three months, and then you eat it,"
said Mr Trevellick, trying to be kind. The butcher gave
him a startled look and so did the other shoppers and
Mr Trevellick hastily opened his little notebook and
pretended to read it.

"Extraordinary!" he said when they were walking
round the small supermarket, "to be able just to go out
and buy food. We either have to grow or raise ours, or
hunt it in the forests. You seem to waste a lot too. Even
the careful Mrs Button throws food away on that little
heap at the bottom of her garden."

"You can't eat potato peelings and rotten cabbage leaves," said Marcus, as usual defending the habits of his own time.

"We haven't discovered the potato yet," said Mr Trevellick, "but we eat everything, otherwise we'd go hungry. In fact in the winter some of us starve. We do manage to pickle some food in salt and water but that gives you a terrible thirst. I shall suggest that we try burying blocks of ice in the ground and keeping meat and vegetables among them. It might work."

All this talk of food had made everyone very hungry by the time they met Mr Snip at twelve-thirty.

"It's my treat, my treat," he said grandly when Marcus tried to pay the bus fares. But when he got out his old leather purse Kate noticed that there wasn't very much money in it.

"I thought we'd go to Hardings," Mr Snip said as they got out at Clapham Junction, "They do an excellent meal there, so I understand." And he led the way into a large restaurant which smelled of boiled cabbage, stewed tea and fried bacon. There were a great many small shiny-topped tables and a long counter running along one wall with dozens of small food lockers at the side of it. On these were printed cards in slots which had written on them things like, *Beans on Toast 1/2, Fish Cakes 2/8, Welsh Rarebit 1/3.*

"It's not very grand I'm afraid," said Mr Snip picking up a tray and taking his place in the long queue which stretched right round the side of the restaurant.

"It's smashing!" said Kate, thinking of the thin purse she had seen, "isn't it Mr Trevellick?"

But Mr Trevellick didn't seem to hear. With that now familiar, dreamy expression in his eyes that the children had come to know so well, he was staring round the steamy restaurant at the other customers. Many of them were old, while the others were either young women with small children or middle-aged ladies in neat but shabby clothes. None of them looked as if they were particularly enjoying their food, and Kate and Marcus knew that they only came to eat in a place like Hardings because they couldn't afford to go anywhere else.

"Mr Trevellick!" said Kate in alarm.

"I can't help it," he said, cracking his knuckles. "I've just got to do something."

"Don't!" implored Marcus.

But it was already too late. Mr Trevellick had shut his eyes and was whispering furiously under his breath.

12. Roast Chicken and Apple Tart

"I THINK I'll have beans on toast," said Mr Snip
reaching out his hand to the steamy little locker, "they're
always very tasty. Quite my favourite food really."

He opened the little door.

"Bless my soul!" he exclaimed, "I do believe they've made a mistake. This isn't beans on toast. It looks more like roast chicken *and* brussel sprouts *and* mashed potatoes *and* bread sauce *and* stuffing." His voice rose higher and higher and then he pulled out his hand and the small door banged shut. Mr Snip put his face right up to the card. It said quite plainly, *Roast Chicken & Extras 10d.*

"How——how very gratifying," said Mr Snip faintly. "I believe I'll change my mind and have the chicken after all." And he pulled out the plate very quickly and put it on his tray.

"You did that," said Marcus in a low voice, frowning at Mr Trevellick who smiled back serenely.

"Come along, come along," said Mr Snip who had now got as far as the puddings and was hesitating between *Apple Tart and Fresh Cream, 4d.* and *Home Made Peach Flan, double portion, 5d.*

"Go on," said Mr Trevellick dreamily. "What's your fancy, Marcus?"

"Fish and chips and vanilla ice with hot chocolate sauce," Marcus said stolidly and got it for 10d. Kate chose chicken and the apple tart and Mr Trevellick got the best Scotch salmon and a three coloured ice-cream.

"And what will you have to drink?" asked Mr Snip as they joined him with their heavily laden trays.

"Ginger beer?" said Marcus looking sideways at Mr Trevellick.

Kate echoed this, and Mr Snip said hopefully to the stout woman who was standing behind the counter with a placid smile on her face, "Two ginger beers, please. Of course, you're not licensed, are you? Otherwise I might ask for something really extravagant, like a glass of sherry."

"Certainly sir," said the woman. "Dry sherry, of course." And she handed him a beautifully cut wine glass full of pale sherry.

"How——how much?" said Mr Snip, almost in a whisper.

"Sixpence, sir," said the woman. She counted up all their food and the bill came to four and fourpence.

"It must be a special Cut Price Day," said Mr Snip, whose hands were shaking so much that Marcus was afraid he would drop his tray. "What wonderful good fortune. I had no idea, no idea at all."

Marcus and Kate, who were quite beyond words, followed him to a corner table, unpacked their trays and sat down.

"And what are you drinking, Mr Trevellick?" asked Mr Snip after five minutes' silent and quite delicious eating.

"Mead," said Mr Trevellick. "I really couldn't resist it."

"Why they've even given me a cigar," said Mr Snip as he finished the very last crumb of peach flan. "It must be a mistake. They never charged me for it. Excuse me one moment." He bustled away to the counter and Marcus licked his already clean ice-cream spoon, put it down and then said accusingly to Mr Trevellick:

"Somebody's bound to start asking questions about this and then . . ."

"There'll be trouble," Mr Trevellick finished for him. "Really! What a boy you are for meeting trouble more than half-way, if I may say so. There was no difficulty over my little meeting with Boadicea was there?"

"No," Marcus agreed reluctantly. He had borrowed Mr Snip's paper every morning since the affair on Westminster Bridge, but there had been no mention at all of the Queen taking the three policemen prisoner.

"Then trust me," said Mr Trevellick grandly. "They will all accept their good fortune as a wonderful stroke of luck."

"All?" said Marcus in a hollow voice.

"All," said Mr Trevellick and waved his arm to embrace the whole restaurant.

At the next table two old age pensioners were contentedly eating pigeon pie for all they were worth. Beyond them a young woman, who had looked distinctly harrassed when Kate had noticed her before, was now beaming happily as she ate a large helping of sherry trifle covered in thick cream, while her three small children were all tucking into enormous helpings of Irish stew. In fact, everybody in the restaurant was now eating his favourite food, and the horrid smell of cabbage and over-stewed tea had disappeared. In its place was the delicious aroma of beautifully cooked meats, exotic spices, rich sauces and crusty pastry.

"They look happier than they did when they were eating the baked beans and the cake of fish, don't they?" said Mr Trevellick, his blue eyes shining.

Mr Snip came hurrying back to tell them that the

cigar was a present from Hardings Management and would he please accept it with their compliments.

"I haven't had one for years," he said. "My word what a lucky chance that we happened to come down here today. I was talking to the woman at the cash desk, charming woman she is too, and she said that it's something to do with Hardings celebrating their centenary."

"It was the nicest lunch I've ever had," said Kate truthfully, for the chicken had been cooked in exactly the way she liked it best and the apple pie had been quite delicious.

"Good, good," said Mr Snip, who was now wreathed in aromatic smoke from his cigar. "If I do something, I do like to do it properly you know. When I was a young man . . ."

He told them at great length exactly what he had been like and ended up with, "Of course we worked hard in those days. I never went gallivanting off, thinking of nothing but enjoying myself, as the young people do now."

"Didn't you even sail a boat on the pond on the Common?" Marcus couldn't help asking.

"Heh, heh, what's that? Nonsense, of course not," said Mr Snip. "Well, we'd better get back, I've got plenty to do you know, arranging my affairs for when I move over to The Haven."

In actual fact he returned to Wandle Heights and went fast asleep in the best armchair with a newspaper over his face. Mr Trevellick started to run up the stairs to his room and Marcus went after him and caught his arm.

"About Mrs Button and this house," he began.

"I know, I know," Mr Trevellick flapped his hands up and down. "I've sent Horace out to the Triangle to start dealing with that."

"But what can he do?" asked Marcus.

"He'll think of something," Mr Trevellick said cheerfully. "And now I simply must get down to work. My time here's running out you know. Why don't you go and join Horace in the garden? Afternoon-afternoon."

"So is Mrs Button's time running out," said Kate when Marcus relayed these rather unhelpful remarks to her. "The cord's gone in my bedroom window and now I can't open it any more. And there are more slates down in the garden; I noticed them yesterday."

"Let's go and talk to Horace," said Marcus.

"He won't talk back to us," said Kate, who like Mr Snip felt very sleepy after her big lunch. "He never does, even though he likes us a bit better now."

She was quite right. The owl turned its back on them quite rudely and refused to say anything, even in Latin. So Marcus and Kate played a rather half-hearted game of hide-and-seek and then sat side by side on the bridge and dangled their feet in the water.

"If Daddy was here, he'd know what to do," said Kate looking at her white wet toes.

"Mr Trevellick's awfully unreliable," said Marcus dolefully. "He does things so suddenly. He gets an idea into his head and then——off he goes before you can stop him."

"Like the pigeons, and Boadicea, and the roast

chicken," said Kate chuckling. "If only we knew what would really make Mrs Button happy, perhaps we could do something to make it come true."

"I wonder if we could," said Marcus shutting his eyes and frowning.

Kate looked up at the whispering willow tree, then at the gleaming beautiful statues, and beyond them at the endless sunny horizon. She felt a little sleepy and very calm and as she sat there with only the sound of the stream to break the silence she had the feeling that the garden itself was trying to speak to her.

"It is an *enchanted* garden after all, "Kate whispered. "Perhaps it would help, even if Mr Trevellick won't."

"I don't see how," said Marcus. "Come on, it must be getting late."

For the next three days Mr Trevellick stayed in his room with the *Please Do Not Disturb* notice hanging on the handle. He came down to meals but his thoughts were obviously elsewhere, and he only smiled vaguely at Marcus when he brought up the subject of Mrs Button.

"It's nearly the end of the holidays, do you realize that?" said Kate on the afternoon of the fourth day. "That means Mr Trevellick'll go back to Ancient Britain and we'll go back to school and Mr Snip'll go to The Haven and then Mrs Button and Miss Button'll be left here all on their own."

"Well, I just don't see what we can do," said Marcus, who had thought and thought until his head seemed to be bursting. He joined Kate at the window and they looked out at the back garden which was nearly invisible as it had grown very dark although it was only three o'clock. A strong wind suddenly blew violently across the Common and all the bushes bowed down before it and the fence creaked. Two of the planks fell onto the flower beds and a moment later there was an awful rending sound and a piece of guttering clattered to the ground right by the glass.

"Are your windows shut?" asked Mrs Button coming slowly into the room. She looked very tired and she was holding onto the door-knob as though she didn't trust herself to stand upright.

"Yes," said Kate, adding in an undertone, "Mine's shut for ever."

"It's going to be a bad storm I'm afraid," said Mrs Button. "Marcus dear, run up and ask Mr Trevellick to shut his window, will you?"

Marcus did as he was asked, but all Mr Trevellick said through the door was, "All right, all right." And then in a lull in the storm Marcus heard the soft scratch, scratch of his pencil stub again.

Mrs Button had spoken the truth. It was a very bad gale while it lasted, and when the wind dropped, the rain started. It came down like a tropical storm. Water found its way through old holes in the roof and dripped through the attic, turning the ceilings in the top rooms into splashy brown and grey maps. It seeped in through the brickwork and ran down the wallpaper, and it splashed off the broken gutter and poured into the garden like a small waterfall.

Kate and Marcus were kept running backwards and

forwards with buckets and cloths and by the end of two hours their legs were aching, but the worst of the damage had been dealt with and the sky was starting to clear. Mrs Button just sat down in the kitchen with her hands folded on the table and stared at the opposite wall.

"Probably the damage isn't too bad," Marcus said.

"No, no I don't suppose it is for a moment," said Mrs Button taking off her steel-rimmed spectacles and rubbing them on her apron.

Marcus looked from the old woman to Kate and then back again. There had been no words from Horace, and Mr Trevellick just wouldn't listen at the moment. Marcus reached a great decision. He went across to the scullery door and opened it and looked out.

"Goodness!" he said loudly. "What has happened to the garden?"

"It's under water I should think," said Mrs Button with the ghost of a smile.

"Do come and look," said Marcus. He took her arm and helped her to her feet, making faces at Kate who was staring at him in bewilderment.

"The Triangle," hissed Marcus. "Come on, and bring a chair. Hurry up."

He led the protesting Mrs Button down the garden to the iron gate at the bottom. He put his hand on the lock and as he did so there was a sweep of wings and Horace flew over their heads.

"We're going into the Triangle," Marcus said loudly.

Horace's yellow eyes gleamed in the soft twilight and

then he wheeled round and flitted away to Mr Trevellick's window.

"You can't!" said Kate, "You know it won't work with other people unless Mr Trevellick's there."

"It's got to," said Marcus.

"It'll vanish for ever," said Kate.

"We'll risk that," replied Marcus and pushed open the gate and led the bewildered Mrs Button through it. "Make Mrs Button happy," he commanded, and then added hastily, "Please."

For a moment they saw the tangled weeds and the ugly broken mattress and the rain-sodden trees, and then they grew fainter and fainter and in their place appeared the beautiful green softly-sunlit garden.

"Oh," said Mrs Button. "Oh, oh, oh."

Kate thoughtfully helped her to sit down on the kitchen chair and Mrs Button said, "Why it's just as it was when I was young."

And as she spoke she *was* young. She was wearing a brown silk dress and her hair was no longer white and all the wrinkles had vanished from her face. And there was somebody with her. A serious-faced man in soldier's uniform who had his cap under his arm and a short swagger-stick in his hand.

"Frederick, dear," said Mrs Button softly. She got up and he put his arm round her waist and she laid her head on his shoulder. "It's been such a very short leave," she said sighing.

"There'll be more," he said. "This war can't last for ever. We'll soon get the Huns on the run, you'll see."

"I hate to think of you out there in France," Mrs Button said.

"I know, dearest."

They were silent for a moment and the children drew back into the shadow of the wall.

"It's Mr Button," Kate whispered.

"Captain Button," Marcus replied. "Shh."

"And when it's all over," the Captain said, "we'll sell the house and move down to Cornwall, just as you've always wanted to."

"And what shall we do with this house?" Mrs Button asked.

"Sell it. It's well built and there'll be a boom in housing after the war. In a nice quiet select neighbourhood like this it'll be worth a fortune. We'll start a little chicken farm and the baby'll grow up in the country and we'll be happy ever after."

"Happy ever after," echoed Mrs Button.

She and her husband strolled down to the stream and as they did so Horace swept over the wall and landed on Marcus' shoulder. He seemed very angry and his yellow eyes were glittering.

"I don't care," said Marcus who understood perfectly why the bird was so cross. "Perhaps we have done everything wrong, but at least Mrs Button's happy for a bit. So there!"

Horace heaved himself up and down and at the same time somebody rattled at the gate.

"Mother, Mother, are you there?" called the voice of Miss Button.

"Oh crikey," said Marcus, "That *has* torn it."

"*In veritus*," agreed Horace furiously. "*Simplicitus, simplicitus, simplicitus!*"

13. The Man from the Council

"I thought I told you," said Mr Trevellick extremely crossly for him, "that I would definitely do
something. Why you're not even apprentices. You don't
begin to understand how to control magic. You can't
even make up a simple nostrum."

"We only wanted to help," said Marcus stubbornly.

"If Horace hadn't been keeping an eye on you and warned me what was happening, things might have been very serious," said Mr Trevellick. "As it is I think we may be able to save something from this disaster."

"We're very sorry," said Kate in a small voice.

"Well it can't be helped," said Mr Trevellick becoming his old cheerful self. "I daresay it was partly my fault too. Only I had to get my reports finished on time. Now leave matters to me."

The moment Marcus had opened the gate to let in the anxious Miss Button, the beautiful garden had vanished as suddenly as if a light had been switched off. Statues, trees, stream and bridge and even the soft evening sky had disappeared, and in their place had been the old familiar overgrown Triangle with Mrs Button sitting on the kitchen chair with her eyes tightly shut and a happy smile on her face.

Miss Button had pushed past the children and run to her mother's side and she was now talking to her in a low anxious voice. She turned to Mr Trevellick and beckoned to him to go and help her; he walked across the muddy, squelchy grass and took Mrs Button gently by the arm and helped her to her feet.

"Really!" said Miss Button, in that high, scolding voice people use when they are very worried, "Fancy coming out here in all this damp with your rheumatism. Whatever possessed you to do such a thing?"

"I really don't know," Mrs Button said, leaning heavily on Mr Trevellick's arm and moving slowly towards the gate where Marcus and Kate were standing. "It was a sudden whim I suppose. I'd been indoors all day and I thought a breath of air might do me good. I must have dozed off for a moment though, because I had such a lovely dream——all about your father's last leave in 1915 before he was killed. I saw him quite, quite clearly——just as he used to be."

"Did you really,"-said Miss Button soothingly. "Well that must have been nice. Come along now, Mother, and I'll make you a good strong cup of tea."

The trio walked slowly past the children towards the house and Marcus hurried back into the Triangle to collect the kitchen chair.

"Well, at least she *was* happy,". Kate said wistfully. "But I suppose we've lost the Triangle for ever."

"We know what she wants," Marcus said, "a chicken farm in Cornwall, though how we're going to get it for her I can't imagine."

They let themselves into the kitchen where the kettle was already starting to sing softly to itself on the stove. Mr Snip was there too, leaning with his back to the door which led through to the passage.

"I didn't know where you'd all gone," he was saying in an aggrieved voice. "I never thought you'd be out in the garden in weather like this. And that reminds me, Mrs Button, the rain's come through the ceiling in my room. I've put a basin under it. And then there was this man banging and banging on the door. *I* didn't know what to do about him."

"What man?" asked Miss Button, swirling hot water round and round in the teapot.

"Some man from the Council. At least he *says* he's from the Council. You can't trust people these days. I've put him in the sitting-room. I hope he hasn't walked off with anything. He looked quite respectably dressed, but you can't be sure."

"I'll go and see him," said Miss Button looking more harrassed than ever, "Kate dear, you make the tea will you?" And she trotted off still wearing her damp hat and coat.

"Tea?" said Mr Snip brightening up. "Now that *is* a good idea."

"There are some biscuits in the tin on the dresser," said Mrs Button who still seemed to be in a happy dream.

Mr Snip dipped his biscuit in his tea and, after a moment's hesitation, Mr Trevellick did the same. He left the biscuit in too long however, so a piece of it melted into the cup, and he was still trying to rescue it with a teaspoon when Miss Button suddenly reappeared with a very flushed face and her hat over one eye.

"He *is* from the Council," she announced, clasping her hands together so that her knuckles went white. "His name's Mr Jenkins and he's ever so nice. He says they want to buy the house."

"This house?" asked Marcus.

"Yes, that's right. He says the Council are going to buy up all the houses round the Triangle to knock them down. Then they're going to build council flats. Fourteen storeys high he says and with central heating and washing machines and everything."

"Lot of new-fangled nonsense," said Mr Snip and then added in alarm, "but what's going to happen to The Haven?"

"Pardon me," said a voice in the doorway, "but if I might say a word perhaps I could assist the gentleman with his enquiry."

"Oh Mr Jenkins I am so sorry," said Miss Button pulling a stoutish young man in a dark suit into the kitchen. "In my excitement I forgot I'd left you out in the passage."

"Not at all, not at all," said Mr Jenkins. "I'm very pleased to meet you all I'm sure. Now then, to deal with the point this gentleman Mr——er? raised."

"Snip," said Mr Snip.

"Quite so. Mr Snip. Well then, sir, set your mind at rest. I have talked to the good lady at The Haven. Quite a cosy chat we had, and she's been making plans for some while it seems to move her——er——household down to Sussex. Penfield is, I believe, the town she mentioned. A charming little place, quiet but not cut off."

"I know it," said Mr Snip. "It's not a bad town. Countrified of course, but you can't have everything."

By which remark everyone gathered that he highly approved of Penfield and was delighted at the news.

"Do have some tea," said Mrs Button, waking slowly from her dream.

"Thank you I'm sure," said Mr Jenkins. "The cup that cheers, as we say in the office, and very welcome on a day like this. Shocking weather. I did come round to see you on Monday, but there was no answer. Two lumps if I may."

"My daughter was at business and everybody else was out so I had a nap," Mrs Button said. "I am sorry that I never heard you."

"Please don't distress yourself on my account," said Mr Jenkins. "And now I'm sure you'd like to know what terms we're offering."

"This house," said Miss Button, putting down her cup and staring rather defiantly at Mr Jenkins, "is not in very good repair. We must be quite honest about that."

"Ah, but that doesn't enter into it, Miss Button," said Mr Jenkins smiling more widely than ever as he wagged a finger at her. "We intend to pull it down you see."

"Yes, I do see," said Miss Button quietly and she sat back in her chair as though a great weight had slipped off her shoulders.

"It's rather sad to think of it being destroyed," said Mrs Button. "I've lived here all my life you know."

"Ah, but we can't stand in the way of progress now can we?" Mr Jenkins said shaking his head. "Now then, I have a paper here which shows exactly what we are offering."

He pulled some documents out of his pocket and Mr Trevellick and the children quietly left the room without anybody noticing. Mr Snip stayed behind, however, partly because he felt that Mrs Button might need a man's support in a business matter, and also because he was extremely curious and did not intend to be left out of anything interesting that was going on.

"Oh, well *done!*" said Marcus out in the hall. "Congratulations, Mr Trevellick."

"Well it was more Horace than me," said Mr Trevellick modestly. "I wanted to do something rather more sweeping. But he kept on finding difficulties——just like you, Marcus——and in the end he convinced me that this was the best way. Of course we had to hurry matters up like anything after you took affairs into your own hands. Mr Jenkins didn't really intend to come here this afternoon, we had to——er——change his mind for him. Your Councils appear to work as slowly as some of our Elders in the Thing."

"How *did* you do it?" asked Kate curiously.

"Trade secret," said Mr Trevellick regretfully. "But one thing you can be sure of and that is that Mrs Button will get a very good price for her house. Horace fixed that. He's quite recovered you know. He says that the Budgic Tonic has done him the world of good and made him feel quite a new owl."

"Have we ruined the Triangle?" Marcus asked.

"I don't think so," Mr Trevellick said cautiously. "But soon, of course, it will disappear for ever. It's a great pity that your civilization has had to build over so many gardens."

"Anyway there's still Trafalgar Square," Marcus said, trying to cheer up Kate. "What luck that nobody built over that."

During the next two days the house was full of people.

Several men came from the Council and went round measuring the walls and the garden, proceedings which interested Marcus a great deal. Mr Snip had Colonel Jackson and Mr Parker over for tea and Miss Button, much to everyone's astonishment, gave in her notice at work.

"I've been with the firm for thirty years," she said, "with never a day off for illness and it's high time I retired and took things a little easier. I shall get a good pension, and what with that and the money the Council are going to pay us, Mother and I will have more than sufficient for our needs."

"Where will you live?" asked Kate.

"Well, the Council did offer us a flat in one of their new blocks," said Miss Button, "but Mother and I talked it over and we decided against it. We're going to buy a nice easy-to-run little bungalow down by the sea somewhere."

"Why not Cornwall?" said Marcus.

"It's funny you should say that," said Miss Button. "Mother and I had exactly the same idea. She always has fancied Cornwall for some reason. How odd that you should suggest it too, Marcus."

"Very odd," agreed Marcus solemnly and went off whistling to talk to the architect who had become quite a friend of his, while Kate caught the bus down to the Junction and did some very important shopping with the last of their holiday pocket money. She also paid a visit to the pet shop where she lingered for a while talking to the puppies and the kittens.

"Hasn't the time whizzed by?" said Marcus on the following day which was the last but one of their holiday.

"I'm awfully sorry that we shan't ever see Mr Trevellick again," said Kate who was very busy tying up an assortment of small parcels.

"So am I, in a way," said Marcus cautiously. "But he *was* awfully difficult to look after. I'll never complain again about having to look after a new boy at school. They aren't half so much trouble."

"Let's ask Mr Trevellick if we can have one more game of hide and seek in the Triangle this afternoon," Kate said, staring out of the window. A grey shape fluttered across the chilly sky and she saw Horace swoop over the wall and begin to fly backwards and forwards across the Triangle as though he was looking for something.

Mr Trevellick applauded the idea enthusiastically.

"Smashing!" he said, throwing his arms about. "Now that I've finished my reports, I could do with some time off myself. Let us go out there immediately after lunch."

"He's up to something," Marcus said suspiciously. "He always gets like that when he's planning."

"Pooh." said Kate, "There isn't time for any more trouble. He goes back to Ancient Britain at midnight."

"Now then," said Mr Trevellick, at two o'clock that afternoon, "in we go. You don't mind, by the way, if Horace comes too? He thought it would be safer."

"Safer for what?" asked Marcus, half in and half out of the Triangle. But Mr Trevellick didn't reply and merely pulled him through the gate. Everything became misty and quiet and a small feathery body suddenly burrowed its way into the front of Marcus' raincoat. And then the mist cleared, but instead of the silent beautiful garden something quite different came into view, and Marcus found himself staring at a rather dirty iron gate. There was a sudden barrage of noise too, people talking and walking about and a great rattling and roaring. A voice said angrily:

"Mind your backs, please."

"Where? What?" said Marcus nimbly dodging to one side as a machine like a great caterpillar banged past him.

"It's Victoria Station," said Kate's voice at Marcus' side.

And it was. The moment she said that, Marcus recognized it instantly and he was so startled he didn't know what to say, or think, or do.

*"*O tempora, O mores!*" said Horace in a muffled voice as he put his head out to look round at the noise and the confusion.

"Yes, but why here?" asked Kate, who was just as startled and frightened as Marcus. Something must have gone dreadfully wrong with the Triangle and there was no sign of Mr Trevellick. Added to which, neither she nor Marcus had any money left for the journey home, as she had spent their last penny on her shopping expedition.

Quite a crowd of people seemed to be gathering round them and a ticket inspector was now standing by the gate leading onto the platform in front of them. A train must have just arrived for hurrying groups began to

*O what times, O what habits.

appear moving towards the barrier and, as Kate stared at them, she suddenly saw a very tall man with a tanned face, who was carrying two battered suitcases covered in labels.

"It's Daddy!" said Kate in a kind of croak.

"It's not fair!" burst out Marcus. "It's a trick. Mr Trevellick is playing some kind of trick on us and it's all just pretend."

"*Pax, pax, simplicitus*," said Horace, squirming round and round.

"It feels real," said Kate who was still staring at the tall man who was only a few yards away now.

"It always does," Marcus said furiously.

And then the tall man was through the barrier and had caught sight of them. His mouth dropped open and his suitcases fell to the ground.

"Well I'm darned!" he said. "What on earth are you two doing here?"

"It *is* Daddy!" shouted Kate and she squirmed through the crowds and put her arms round her father's waist and hugged him violently.

"Well, I don't know," said Mr Dawson, "I really don't. How did you find out that I was coming back today and on this very train? I haven't let anyone know in advance because I wanted it to be a surprise."

"You mean you're really you?" Marcus asked.

"I hope so," Mr Dawson said, ruffling his head. "I don't feel at all like anybody else. I finished my job far sooner than I expected, you see, and when I cabled Head Office they told me to come back right away to discuss a new job. They want to promote me and that means I'd be working here in England from now on. What do you think of that eh?"

"It's super!" said Kate breathlessly. "It's the nicest thing that's ever happened to us, isn't it Marcus?"

"Yes," said Marcus huskily, and as he bent down to pick up one of the suitcases he whispered, "Thank you, Horace, thank you very much. Oh you——you *rara avis.*"

Horace tried to look modest and failed completely.

★*"Vulgo enim dicitur: Iucundi acti labores,"* he said complacently.

*For it is commonly said: accomplished labours are pleasant.

14. The Garden Vanishes

"I'm sorry he's going," said Mr Snip. "Strange feller, but there's something rather nice about him really."

"We're going to see him off," said Kate.

"He'll be catching the midnight train I suppose," said

Mr Snip, consulting his watch. "Well, he'd better look smart about it; the buses aren't too reliable at this time of night. And talking of time, young lady, shouldn't you two be in bed by now? When I was your age...".

"We're just going to say goodbye to Mr Trevellick," Marcus was saying to his father out in the hall. "We won't be long."

"I'm sorry I shan't be able to see more of him," said Mr Dawson. "He seems to have become a great friend of yours."

"Yes," said Marcus, who nevertheless couldn't help feeling secretly relieved that his father couldn't get to know Mr Trevellick better. Mr Dawson went into the sitting-room to join the Buttons and Mr Snip while Kate slipped out. The door closed and a pleasant murmur of talk began behind it as Mr Trevellick came slowly down the stairs carrying his heavy leather case.

In silence the three of them tip-toed down the passage, through the kitchen and the scullery and out into the back garden. It was a fine moonlit night, bathed as usual in the strange orange glow from the street lamps. Horace shut his eyes and burrowed further into Mr Trevellick's pocket. A train thundered through the cutting; somewhere a television set was turned up rather too high, and a bus squelched to a halt on the corner.

Mr Trevellick paused with his hand on the iron gate leading into the Triangle. His face looked unusually pale and his bright blue eyes although excited were also a little sad.

"We've never really thanked you properly," Kate said.

"No, no," said Mr Trevellick earnestly, "it is I who am in your debt. Without you I should have been lost."

"I do hope you pass your exams all right," said Marcus.

"A fully fledged member of the M.A.T." said Mr Trevellick dreamily. "Everything will have been worth it if I achieve that."

"We've brought you some presents," said Kate, pulling some parcels out of her raincoat pocket. "There are six packets of soup for your mother, Mr Trevellick, with our love. I chose the ones which had the prettiest pictures on them. And for Horace there are two bottles of Budgies' Tonic, and for you a ball-point pen with three refills. I would have got more but we ran out of money. It's a very good pen."

"How very kind," said Mr Trevellick huskily. "They will be quite astounded at the next meeting of the Circle when I show them that. We've never had anything so remarkable since somebody bequeathed us part of Odin's drinking horn. I really don't know what to say."

There was a short, rather shy silence while Mr Trevellick carefully put the presents in his case together with his papers and potions and the hour-glass.

"Well, then, it's goodbye," said Mr Trevellick.

They shook hands rather sadly and Horace fluttered onto Mr Trevellick's shoulder and cleared his throat.

*"*Cras ingens iterabimus aequor*," he said and then added, "as it happens I've quite taken to you two. As children go, you're really not too bad."

*Tomorrow we set out once more upon the boundless sea.

"He spoke to us in English," said Kate in an awed voice.

"A sign of great distinction," said Mr Trevellick giving her the ghost of a wink. "Goodbye Marcus, goodbye Kate. And again my very deepest thanks."

He pushed open the gate as he spoke and, as he did so, the children caught a glimpse of tall trees surrounding a clearing where several stately gentlemen with white beards and long clothes were standing. Beyond them was a brilliant blue sky and a sea that sparkled and burst into foam against dark rocks. And the air was full of the scent of flowers and grass and salt.

"Come back and see us again," called Kate and Marcus added, "Yes, do please. And the best of luck with MAT."

"Thank you, I'll try," said Mr Trevellick and then a dark mist rolled across in front of them and there was nothing to see but the gate clanging shut.

"What are you doing out here," said Mr Dawson, coming down the garden path towards them.

"We came out for a breath of air," said Marcus.

"It's high time you were both in bed," said Mr Dawson taking their cold hands in his. "Well, has Mr Trevellick gone?"

"Quite gone," said Kate with a small sigh. "You see, Daddy, he didn't have to catch a train at all. He used the magic garden. Look," and she pulled back the curtain of ivy leaves.

Mr Dawson obligingly glanced through the railings of the iron gate at the damp, bare trees and the tangled grass and the broken mattress.

"I see," he said gravely. "That's most interesting. Now come on you two, you can do the rest of your dreaming in bed."

"But," said Kate.

"Mr Trevellick was . . ." said Marcus.

"Yes, yes," said Mr Dawson, "You can tell me all about your games in the morning."

And with those words he led them up the bumpy garden path away from the Triangle and back to Number Four Wandle Heights.

FAIRY FANTASY

Maria Gripe
112288 THE GLASSBLOWER'S CHILDREN 45p

GIRLS' ROMANTIC FICTION

Ruth M. Arthur
111648 THE AUTUMN GHOSTS 50p
111729 THE CANDLEMAS MYSTERY 45p*

HOBBY BOOKS (NF)

Christopher Reynolds
10823X CREATURES OF THE BAY (illus) 50p
100573 THE POND ON MY
WINDOW-SILL (illus) 30p
David Shaw
112369 CRAFTS FOR GIRLS 50p

0426 LIFE STORIES

John Rowland
104013 ROCKET TO FAME (NF) (illus) 25p

MAGIC AND FAMILY STORIES

Nina Beachcroft
103564 WELL MET BY WITCHLIGHT 30p
Helen Cresswell
108825 THE WHITE SEA HORSE
and Other Sea Magic (illus) 35p
Eleanor Estes
107519 THE WITCH FAMILY (illus) 50p*
Margaret Greaves
10305X STONE OF TERROR 30p
Elizabeth Gundrey
108906 THE SUMMER BOOK (NF) (illus) 45p
Mollie Hunter
113756 THE WALKING STONES 45p*
Spike Milligan
105672 BAD JELLY THE WITCH (illus) 60p
109546 DIP THE PUPPY (illus) 60p
Hilary Seton
106989 THE HUMBLES (illus) 50p
109112 THE NOEL STREATFIELD CHRISTMAS
HOLIDAY BOOK (illus) 40p
109031 THE NOEL STREATFIELD EASTER
HOLIDAY BOOK (illus) 45p
105249 THE NOEL STREATFIELD SUMMER
HOLIDAY BOOK (illus) 50p

*Not for sale in Canada

MYSTERY

Tim Dinsdale
105915 **THE STORY OF THE
LOCH NESS MONSTER** 50p

Leonard Gribble
104285 **FAMOUS HISTORICAL
MYSTERIES** (NF) (illus) 35p

Alfred Hitchcock (Editor)
117387 **ALFRED HITCHCOCK'S TALES OF
TERROR AND SUSPENSE** 60p

Bernhardt J. Hurwood
105591 **HAUNTED HOUSES** (NF) (illus) 30p

108310 **VAMPIRES, WEREWOLVES AND
OTHER DEMONS** 30p

Larry Kettelkamp
102681 **INVESTIGATING
GODS** (NF) (illus) 30p

113594 **INVESTIGATING
UFOs** (NF) (illus) 35p

QUIZ, HUMOUR AND FUN BOOKS

Brad Anderson
115864 **MARMADUKE** 35p*

115945 **MORE MARMADUKE** 35p*

116070 **MARMADUKE RIDES AGAIN** 35p

Nicola Davies
102843 **THE TARGET BOOK OF FUN AND
GAMES** (NF) (illus) 50p

10532X **THE 2nd TARGET BOOK OF FUN
AND GAMES** (NF) (illus) 30p

103465 **THE 3rd TARGET BOOK OF FUN
AND GAMES** (NF) (illus) 50p

115198 **THE TARGET BOOK OF
JOKES** (NF) 40p

Carey Miller
114396 **THE TARGET BOOK OF
FATE & FORTUNE** 50p

Nils-Olof Franzen
108078 **AGATON SAX AND THE LEAGUE
OF SILENT EXPLODERS** 40p

107942 **AGATON SEX AND THE LONDON
COMPUTER PLOT** (illus) 30p

Christine Nostlinger
107438 **THE CUCUMBER KING** 45p

103483 **PETER PIPPIN'S 3rd BOOK OF
PUZZLES** (NF) (illus) 30p

D & C Power
117115 **THE TARGET BOOK OF
PICTURE PUZZLES** 40p

R.W.Wilson
104366 **THE LONDON QUIZ
BOOK** (NF) (illus) 40p

*Not for sale in Canada

CHILDREN'S BOOKS

0426	TARGET		

ADVENTURE

	Graeme Cook		
105087	**COMMANDOS IN ACTION!**	(illus) (NF)	35p
	Terrance Dicks		
110927	**THE MOUNTIES: THE GREAT MARCH WEST**		40p
111052	**THE MOUNTIES: MASSACRE IN THE HILLS**		40p
111133	**THE MOUNTIES: WAR DRUMS OF THE BLACKFOOT**		45p
	Rex Edwards		
105400	**ARTHUR OF THE BRITONS**		40p
	G. Krishnamurti		
103645	**THE ADVENTURES OF RAMA**		35p
	John Lucarotti		
11535X	**OPERATION PATCH**		45p

ANIMAL STORIES

	Judith M. Berrisford		
107004	**SKIPPER AND SON**	(illus)	35p
107195	**SKIPPER AND THE RUNAWAY BOY**	(illus)	35p
107276	**SKIPPER'S EXCITING SUMMER**		40p
	Molly Burkett		
111567	**THAT MAD, BAD BADGER . . .**	(NF)	35p
	Constance Taber Colby		
109899	**A SKUNK IN THE FAMILY**	(illus) (NF)	45p
	G. D. Griffiths		
113675	**ABANDONED!**	(illus)	35p
	David Gross		
117549	**THE BADGERS OF BADGER HILL**		50p
	Sara Herbert		
109627	**THE PONY PLOT**		35p
109708	**THE SECRET OF THE MISSING FOAL**		35p
	Alex Lea		
107861	**TEMBA DAWN, MY CALF**		30p
	Joyce Stranger		
11017X	**THE SECRET HERDS**	(illus)	45p
	Alison Thomas		
115511	**BENJI**		40p

CHILDREN'S BOOKS

0426	'DOCTOR WHO'	
116151	Terrance Dicks & Malcolm Hulke **THE MAKING OF DOCTOR WHO**	60p
114558	Terrance Dicks **DOCTOR WHO AND THE ABOMINABLE SNOWMAN**	40p
112954	Terrance Dicks **DOCTOR WHO AND THE AUTON INVASION** (illus)	40p
110250	Terrance Dicks **DOCTOR WHO AND THE CARNIVAL OF MONSTERS**	50p
11471X	Malcolm Hulke **DOCTOR WHO AND THE CAVE MONSTERS**	40p
117034	Terrance Dicks **DOCTOR WHO AND THE CLAWS OF AXOS**	50p*
113160	David Whittaker **DOCTOR WHO AND THE CRUSADERS** (illus)	40p
114981	Brian Hayles **DOCTOR WHO AND THE CURSE OF PELADON**	40p
114639	Gerry Davis **DOCTOR WHO AND THE CYBERMEN**	40p
113322	Barry Letts **DOCTOR WHO AND THE DAEMONS** (illus)	40p
112873	David Whitaker **DOCTOR WHO AND THE DALEKS** (illus)	40p
11244X	Terrance Dicks **DOCTOR WHO AND THE DALEK INVASION OF EARTH**	50p*
118421	Terrance Dicks **DOCTOR WHO DINOSAUR BOOK**	75p
108744	Malcolm Hulke **DOCTOR WHO AND THE DINOSAUR INVASION**	40p

*Not for sale in Canada

Wyndham Books are obtainable from many booksellers and newsagents. If you have any difficulty please send purchase price plus postage on the scale below to:

Wyndham Cash Sales,
123 King Street,
London W6 9JG

While every effort is made to keep prices low, it is sometimes necessary to increase prices at short notice. Wyndham Books reserve the right to show new retail prices on covers which may differ from those advertised in the text or elsewhere.

Postage and Packing Rate.
U.K. & Eire
One book 15p plus 7p per copy for each additional book ordered to a maximum charge of 57p.

These charges are subject to Post Office charge fluctuations.